HERO'S
WALK

By ROBERT CRANE

Ballantine Books • **New York**

For Pierre Bourdelle

1

SUDDENLY he was afraid of glass.

It came upon him in the elevator without any warning, a vestigial memory perhaps, or the recollection of something he had read many years ago, a line in an old chronicle: the fear of glass. The entire building was sheathed in glass (an example of the architectural idealism that inspired the Palace of InterCos) so that men outside could at all times look in, and men inside could at all times look out. From the outside you could see men and women of all races working together for the good of humanity; from the inside you could look out at the world and its people, at the sky and its stars. And in the past he had felt pleasure at working inside this glass sheath, this immense dedicated structure, for glass—held tightly in its place—was a noble material. It was functional and beautiful. It was physically and spiritually hygienic.

But glass could cease to be noble, cease to be conventionally functional, glass could go mad, glass could go whirling through the air like the instrument of an executioner, slashing the flesh open, amputating arms and legs, gouging out an eye, it could slice like a beheading ax, it could drive in slivers through the body like a shower of spears. It was too brittle, it was too irresponsible, it was too murderous at certain moments in history, and he wanted to get away from it. He felt as if he were in a glass-enclosed vacuum which might implode upon him without warning, all sixty stories shattering like a monstrous cathode-ray tube, tearing and slashing and leaving only some gruesome little fragment of himself still alive still quivering.

The fear was very real. He could do nothing to quell it. As the elevator descended in the glass shaft he was trembling slightly. When the glass doors slid open on the ground floor he hesitated before he stepped out. In order to reach the North exit where his car was parked he had to walk through a long corridor—a glass corridor. The walls on either side were immense undivided panes, thirty feet high, a hundred and fifty feet long; and in a strong wind you could see these walls flexing, the surfaces would bulge and waver, shining with the most delicate iridescent colors. They had been donated by the Pan-Arabian Federation four years ago, when the building was being erected; and in one corner of one wall an inscription had been etched:

For the Palace of InterCos
from the People of Arabia
Through the Sands of our Desert
Behold the Sands of Our Universe
June 2016

He began to walk from the elevator to the eastern exit, ashamed of his fear and this unprecedented lack of control. He found that his lungs were tight, his arms were stiff, his skin had become rough and cold and painfully sensitive; there was a momentary time lag in all his movements—he could feel (for the first time in his life) the motor centers in his brain ordering his legs to go forward and the fractional reluctance of his legs to obey the commands. *Damned glass everywhere,* a harsh voice inside him kept crying: *Damned glass, damned glass,* and another voice said uneasily in response, *Don't be such a fool, nothing's going to happen, nothing.* The harsh voice, though, was more influential: he was wildly conscious of those gleaming Arabian walls, he was waiting every instant for the sound of their shattering and the terrible downpour of splinters, and he could smell the sweat of fear under his armpits. Glass. He forced himself as he walked, to look through the interior wall on his right, at the secretarial offices; and he saw without any surprise that they were brightly lit but empty. This morning they had been filled with girls, puzzled and apprehensive but busy, at work. Now: empty. He walked on a few yards and forced himself to look out, through the exterior wall on his left; and he saw that the Grand Plaza was empty too, except for a handful of people who stood far back (away from the glass) staring vacantly at the transparent building. Usually there were thousands of people out there gaping at the fountains, at the statues, at the replicas of famous rockets, at all the brilliant pageantry of InterCos. The flags were still flying, he noticed, the fountains were playing their interminable quadrille; the floodlights had already been turned on, as they always were, half an hour before sunset; the massive centerpiece of the Grand Plaza, the Ad Astra, still soared magnificently, an overpowering silhouette against the darkening sky; and it was all exactly as he had seen it innumerable times before—the most beautiful, the most dramatic vista built by the hands of man, only empty. Lifeless. Deserted. Humanity had abandoned it, leaving just this handful of people to watch beyond the range of falling glass. *To watch for what?* he asked himself savagely. *What do they expect?*

He was halfway to the exit now. *Hurry,* the harsh voice cried inside him: *Damned glass. Hurry.* He tried not to hurry. He tried to walk slowly, with dignity, as became a member of the United States Delegation in InterCos. Ahead of him he saw that the guards had gathered together in the foyer, and it was somehow important to give them the impression that he was in full command of himself, today was no different from yesterday or the day before. The guards were standing well back, as far as possible from the glass walls of the Arabian corridor and the glass doors of the exit; they were huddled like cattle in a rainstorm. They felt the same fear, he realized; probably the entire human race felt the same fear. Glass! A new phobia, acquired in a few hours. Look down from your shining tower, O Lords of InterCos, and see what has happened to your people! *Glass!*

The walls of the foyer were marble, white with superb black veining, as lofty, as impressive as the Arabian glass walls, but infinitely less lethal. The guards watched in silence as he approached, their faces pale and inquisitive, and he knew that they clearly recognized his fear (as he had recognized theirs): they could see fear in the unnaturally jaunty steps he took, in the stiffly held body, the irregular echo of his progress; and again he was angry and ashamed, as if his manhood had turned rotten in public view. The coward inside his brain was hurrying, hurrying to reach the safety of those marble walls; and he was unable to control or even argue with the coward, the harsh driving voice. *Hurry! The glass avalanche might crash down this instant! Hurry!* Another few yards, another few yards; and he was there. He was momentarily safe.

The guards were staring at him, as if he had walked unscratched through the eye of a mysterious catastrophe —a cavern of burning ice, or a silent and invisible tornado. They were tall men, very handsome in their Inter-Cos uniforms, blue, gold buttons, gold helmet, white buckskin boots. He had no wish to speak to them, and there was no need today to sign the Delegation book. As he came abreast of them he steadied himself, said briefly, "Good night," and turned to go through the doors.

"Mr. Harrison."

He turned again, irritably. "Yes?"

The man who spoke was a big Irishman named Luxley.

"Are you leaving then, Mr. Harrison?"

"Yes."

"God Almighty, sir, you won't get far."

"Why not?"

"Every street in the city is blocked, sir. It's a madhouse out there."

"I know," he said. "I saw the newscast a few minutes ago."

4

Another guard said,"It's chaos, Mr. Harrison. Inconceivable chaos." He was a Russian.

"You'd be better off to stay here the night," Luxley said. "Believe me, sir. Besides which——." He looked out at the Grand Plaza and up at the sky. "We've waited the full two hours. It's time for another packet of the things."

"They come every two hours," a Chinese guard said somberly.

"Devils," the Irishman said. "Mr. Harrison, are they devils up there or not, sending those things at us?"

"Aggressors," the Russian said. "We should have no mercy on them. Not an ounce of mercy."

"Glass is the worst thing," a West Indian guard said. "Did you hear what happened on Madison Avenue, Mr. Harrison?"

"Nine young girls," Luxley said vehemently. "God help us, nine young girls, cut to ribbons—are you going, sir?"

"Yes."

They all wanted to talk, pointlessly, passionately, pouring out words to relieve their anxieties. He recalled what his brother Mark had said last night: *The human race has not experienced bombardment for eighty years. We don't know how people will take it.* This was how they took it. A sudden wild phobia (glass) and a babble of words. He had no wish to listen, and he repeated "Good night," and went to the door.

"What is happening in the Council of Ministers?" the West Indian guard asked quickly.

"What is Dr. Werner doing?" the Russian demanded; and the Chinese asked, "What is the Lord Hsuen doing?"

He shook his head regretfully and walked out. *Those are good questions,* he said to himself as the doors revolved. *Those are exceedingly good questions, what is Dr. Werner doing, what is the Lord Hsuen doing, what is happening in the Council of Ministers. Unfortunately, I cannot give, I do not know the answers. Probably they are as frightened as everybody else, possibly they are just sitting and staring at the glass walls and the glass dome of the Council Chamber, wondering when the avalanche*

5

*will descend on them, waiting for the roar of the vacuum
imploding. . . .*

The evening air was cool. The sun had already set and
a pale-red glow remained on the horizon, far to the
west, over the flatlands of New Jersey. He could smell
the strange new odor that had come to the city—the
stench of the green metallic fungus on the Hudson; it
was stronger now than it had been in the morning or at
midday. There had been bulletins about the stuff every
few minutes in all the Delegation offices, detailing its
rapid spread. Here it had not yet reached either shore,
but in the Pool of London and on the Seine it was in
contact with land, burning its way like acid through anything it touched. "We are facing a new technology," Dr.
Werner had said at one of the afternoon conferences.
"A new and unusual and in some ways alarming technology. But, gentlemen, I urge you not to lose heart.
Everything in our power is being done, and if we remain
calm, if we approach the problems judiciously, with
confidence, we can be sure that. . . ."

Words, he had thought even at the time. The words
of desperation. Now, smelling the fungus on the evening
air, he thought again, angrily and contemptuously,
Words.

He walked a few steps and paused to look back at the
Palace of InterCos. It was fantastically beautiful. From
here the glass lost most of its menace, it was no longer
colorless, brittle, on the point of disintegrating. He could
not imagine this lovely structure changed in any way.
There was softness and depth in the glass, reflections of
the night sky—dark blues and greens, purple and the
glowing red of the horizon; there were patterns of dancing light sparkling up from the floodlit fountains and
warmer color reflected from the flags in the Grand Plaza.
"Our jewel box, truly," Dr. Werner had once said of it:
"Holding man's wildest and most exciting dreams."

He turned to walk on. Luxley, the Irish guard, called
to him and came running over, breathing heavily.

"Mr. Harrison," he said, "by God—excuse the pro-
fanity, sir—you're right. I'd rather die out here in the

6

open than back there like a cat in a sack." He took off his gold helmet and rubbed his hair with the palm of his hand. "Faugh," he said. "Do you smell the stink of that copper algae? Algae—is that the name for it?"

"I guess that's as good a name as any."

"It's horrible stuff. I'll walk you to your car and keep you company, sir."

"Thanks."

"It's one of those Iranian cars, isn't it? Lovely little jobs they are, all covered with that fancy engraving."

"Yes."

"So I thought," Luxley said. He was nervous, breathless, but apparently determined to show that he had courage too. He laughed and said, "It's a pleasure to stretch your legs, isn't that a fact?"

"Yes."

They had gone only a few yards when the earth began to shake. They stopped, frozen, counting the thuds, feeling the explosions through their feet and their knees, up through their bellies and their lungs, eyes, brains. Nine thuds. Nine reverberations.

"Nine," the Irishman said weakly. "Did you count them?"

"Nine."

"Thank the Lord, they were way off. In the Bronx, I reckon, or Harlem. No damage done."

"No damage done here."

"A good way off," Luxley repeated, and began to laugh. "And what do you think of that? They're keeping it up. The ninth bloody salvo, the devils, and they send over nine bloody bombs. It proves they can count."

"A nice simple arithmetical progression."

"Is that what you call it, sir?"

"Yes. Let's go."

They went on toward the car park. He was shaking, not so much with fear now as with horror at this last attack. It was distant but it was aimed at human beings, and he could hardly bear to think of what might have happened—the glass shattered, men, women, and children maimed, the gruesome little fragments still alive, still

7

quivering. And yet the tension inside him had broken. He was shaking, every nerve was raw, but with moral indignation, not with personal agony. He realized that for the last ten or twenty minutes he had been waiting for this salvo; while he was walking through the glass corridor he had been expecting it to crash down upon him.

"How far do you have to go, sir?"

"Sixtieth and Fifth."

"That's not so far," Luxley said. He was shaking too, and yet there was relief in his voice. "You'll have plenty of time to make it. The next packet won't be for another two hours."

"Yes," Neil began; but they were both wrong and there was no time left for further conversation. The night air, in one convulsive moment, grew black, the ground seemed to open, the world was illuminated by a great flash of orange light that was gone in an instant, leaving a darker blackness, there was a tremendous burst of wind and this wind was also noise, reverberating up into the sky in wave after wave, with a shrill scream trailing up beyond the thunder. He heard, far, far away, Luxley shout, "Look out!" and he heard the sound he had so long been dreading, the endless fracturing of glass; inside his head a voice called his own name, "Harrison! Neil Harrison!" and there were other explosions that in some strange manner he counted, adding them up to ten, all accompanied by the same reverberations mounting up to the sky and the same diminishing shriek.

Then it was over, except for the continued noise of glass, and he found himself crawling on the ground, on the smooth concrete, saying, "Libby, Libby. Libby Hewes, Libby." In fact, he was trying to find the Irishman.

In a few moments he made the discovery—somehow more terrifying—that he had been not in the very heart of the salvo but only on the fringe of it. The nearest missile had landed two or three hundred yards away and had started several fires: he could see the flames stabbing up

8

into a cloud of swirling brown smoke. Beyond, to the right and to the left, there were other nuclei of flame where other missiles had struck, and it was like looking across at a nightmarish landscape, a panorama of burning slag heaps in an unfamiliar country. *How did it feel in the center of the salvo?* he thought wildly.

He found the Irishman only a few yards away, hunched on the ground, and for a moment he thought the man was dead. He bent down to touch him, and to his amazement Luxley sprang up, his helmet awry, and began to run like a rabbit toward the glass building, dodging from side to side. He stopped suddenly and shouted, "Come back, sir. For God's sake, Mr. Harrison, come on back."

Neil stood unmoving.

"You'll be killed out there," the big man bawled. "They mean to kill every one of us. Don't be a fool." He waited impatiently, and then flapped his arms in a gesture of wild despair and went running on, leaping awkwardly over the debris in his way.

Neil watched. He raised his eyes and looked up at the dirty yellow smoke that was already drifting around the glass walls of the Palace of InterCos, at the reflected streamers of fire, and he could discern no evidence of damage: the glass, after all, had survived the blast from the nearest missile. He wondered what Dr. Werner was thinking at this moment, what the Lord Hsuen and the Prince Dhevu and Crandall and the other members of the Council were thinking, what messages were coming from Washington, London, Peking, Moscow, and what the Voices were saying. He wondered whether his brother Mark was safe, and Mark's wife Evelyn; and he shook with terror picturing Libby alone in her apartment.

Finally he said to himself, "I must get to her," and turned away from InterCos. His mind was full of confusion, memories of things seen and things heard and things felt. Dr. Werner kept reappearing like a figure on a three-dimensional telescreen, and Neil heard him talking constantly about the Beta Complex, and about

9

the time schedule, and about the instruments of a purpose *(we, the instruments of a purpose, we).* But over the sound of his words was always the sound of Voices, a passionate shouting very far away. . . . *NE . . . NE . . . ne . . . kommen . . . ne kommen . . . NE . . . NE . . . marzzzh . . . parzzzh . . . NE . . . NE . . . ne . . . nek-k-k-kommen. . . .*

He found that he was acting stupidly, as if he were drunk or half-asleep, walking directly toward the fires instead of away from them; and he realized that he was continuing to walk to the car park and he had even taken the car keys out of his pocket and was jingling them in his hand. There must have been some dim crazy notion in his mind that he could still get to his car, still drive swiftly to Libby's apartment, although he had seen on the newscast (only a few minutes ago) that all the avenues, all the streets, all the exits from the city were blocked with stalled traffic. Some enterprising reporter hard at work had thought it worth while to picture the scene from the air—a scoop!—people frantically trying to reach the airports, trying to reach the Jersey side of the Hudson or the Long Island side of the East River, trying to reach any place away from the bombardment. They had only succeeded in jamming themselves into a solid immovable mass; and the newly appointed Director of Public Safety at InterCos was imploring them to go home. "Go home, go home, you'll be safer at home——"

He walked on hopelessly, compelled to find the heart of the fires, as if he had to see them with his own eyes to be convinced that they were real, that he was actually living through this scene. The air was nauseatingly thick, brown with smoke and dirt, sour-sweet from the fumes of explosive and whatever was burning ahead. He began to retch and put his handkerchief over his nose and mouth; and he ducked involuntarily once or twice as sheets of ash came floating over him, settling slowly like charred parachutes. Curious chunks of debris littered his way, masses of foamed white plastic, wheels, large

10

jagged slabs of transparent material, crumpled sheets of metal, burst cushions with the stuffing hanging out; and at last he was aware that it was the car park itself that had been hit, this debris came from cars that had been blown to pieces, the flames came from cars that were burning.

When he entered the car park he saw it all clearly. The missile had hit near the edge, and the cars had been flung in all directions. They were piled in heaps; and the heaps were blazing. There was a deep crater where the missile had penetrated, and there were fragments of cars within this crater and other cars were tilted over the rim. The booth at the entrance was shattered, and an attendant in an InterCos uniform was sitting peacefully dead in the ruins, his head tilted to one side as if he were dreaming, but another attendant lay beside him horribly dead, his body torn apart by the axle from one of the cars. He saw a man in a car nearby, a man in a white suit who seemed to be unhurt and was looking at him in a dazed appealing way; and he recognized the man—Thorens, from the Dutch delegation. He said loudly, "Thorens!" and hurried over to the car, pulled the door open and tried to help him out; but the man continued to sit, holding the wheel, staring at Neil, and as Neil took his arm he fell sideways as if all his bones had turned to pulp. *Blast*, Neil thought vaguely: *Isn't it blast that kills like that?* He remembered reading about it in a book. Blast: air rushing out and rushing back again.

Somebody was coming toward him, another InterCos attendant, his gold helmet in his hand, his white tunic stained with oil. He limped over to Neil and said, "Pass, please. All passes must be shown before entering cars." Neil saw that he was mad; not violently, but dully mad. "It was a big black bird," the attendant said. "It flew right over my head just like that. Pass, please. I can't let you in without you show me your pass." He suddenly pointed at the dead attendant, the peaceful one, and screamed, "Look at Franklin, sitting down on the job. Why isn't Franklin working like me?"

Neil took him by the shoulder and led him a few paces

11

away. "Go back to the main building," he said gently. "They'll take care of you there."

The man waddled off and turned, bright-eyed. "Show Franklin your pass," he called and chuckled. "Franklin will check you out. Lazy dog."

Neil watched him go, watched him waver into the smoke, and then looked at the graveyard scene again. His car, the little Iranian sports car of which he was so fond and so proud, was near the crater, where a dozen cars lay mangled and glowing. As he watched, something crumbled and flames spurted out, showers of sparks flew into the air. Momentarily he was alarmed, but the alarm trickled away almost immediately. He heard a helicopter whirring overhead, that same reporter still hard at work, no doubt; and he wondered how the scene looked on the screens of the Delegation office. He had to get to Libby; but in his heart he was sure that he would never reach her tonight: the eleventh salvo, the twelfth, the twentieth, the fiftieth, still had to fall and he would not escape all of them. Nevertheless, it was necessary to try to reach her. He began to walk through the car park to the exit on the far side.

2

FOUR days ago, when there were no missiles and no
fires and no metallic green fungus, the Council of Ministers had met in General Session at the Palace of Inter-
Cos. The Voices, at this time, had been heard for nearly
a year, but they were not the important issues with which
the Council of Ministers was due to concern itself. Dr.
Werner, however, was expected to discuss them in the
course of the session.

Officially the meeting had been called for purely ad-
ministrative reasons: to approve the time schedule for
the dispatch, final assembly and launching of the Beta
Complex, which had become popularly known as Platform Beta. Beta was practically ready to go into operation. Most of the sections had been transported to New
Panama, via Platform Alpha, during the past three years;
and the engineers in New Panama were awaiting the
final sections, including the reactors and control chamb-
ers. These, completed, stood ready for dispatch at the
two major InterCos workshops, Sahara and Lake Baikal.
Planning Division at InterCos had circulated a memorandum to each delegation ahead of the meeting, giving
all relevant information about the present status of Beta,
with the estimated schedule which the Council was expected to approve. Forty-seven days had been allotted
for delivery to New Panama, another forty-seven days
for assembly, eleven days more for launching preparations and tests, three days for Beta to travel to its orbit.

In three and a half months, therefore, Beta could be circling Mars, with its own fully equipped workshops and its own stabilized launching site. These were the mechanical facts of the situation. In normal circumstances Dr. Werner would simply have announced the firing date, after consultation with the Senior Engineers and the appropriate subcommittees, and the Council of Ministers would have approved it by a voice vote.

But the circumstances were not altogether normal. Even four days ago, in a world that was seemingly prosperous, confident and at peace, there were disturbing crosscurrents. The Ministers assembled in an atmosphere of crisis—and not one crisis but a mass of disagreements and irritations, related and unrelated. For example, there had been another violent clash between China and India over colonization quotas for Mars; and the British and Americans—hopelessly outnumbered in the Council —were striving for new discussions on the whole subject of colonization policy. There had been an unexpected quarrel between Australia and Russia over patrol craft zones from Platform Alpha to New Panama. The Arabs were restless for a number of reasons—the Sahara workshop was draining off much needed power, and they were also suffering from a sense of offended dignity because of the way InterCos had handled a dispute with the Turks. The Danes were annoyed with the Swedes, and the Portuguese with the Spaniards. Some of these issues were trivial, some were grave; but they were all likely to be raised at this General Session. The launching of Beta, which the majority of the Ministers would undoubtedly approve over British and American objections, might be delayed, unless Dr. Werner was able to work his magic and restore harmony among the delegates.

The widespread uneasiness was seen at once, as soon as the General Session opened. Many of the Ministers had requested assistance from their governments: Sir Alton Berkeley had flown over from London to sit with his Minister, Goeffrey Vernon; SecState Lowell had flown from Washington to sit in with the American Minister, Crandall, who was Neil's chief. Even the Lord Hsuen

14

was accompanied by Ai-Wen-Tai, the venerable and strange old woman who was unofficially one of the seven rulers of China. The Russian, Balatov, was flanked by two men whom Neil had never seen before. The Prince Dhevu sat with his sister, a young girl with features like a hawk. And there was throughout the assembly a feeling of strain, of fatigue, as if everybody had spent the previous night arguing. SecState Lowell, usually imperturbable, was pale. Crandall was jittery. Both Dhevu and Hsuen looked restless.

The meeting was held in the great Council Chamber, high under the roof of InterCos. It was a place that Neil loved, huge, airy, immaculate, beautifully adapted to its purpose—the debate of man's most passionate dreams. The walls and the domed ceiling were glass, so although they were covered with murals the world outside was never completely closed out, you were always conscious (as the designers intended) of the sky, of day and night, of the sun and the wind and the wheeling planets. The majestic panorama of the Universe always seeped in to remind the President and the Ministers and their aides that they were only the instruments of a purpose.

The instruments of a purpose. This, as everybody expected, was the theme of Dr. Werner's opening address. He looked very impressive on the podium as he smiled down at the semicircle of delegates, a tall handsome man who might have stepped out of a painting by Velasquez: silver-gray hair that curled over his temples, a narrow oval face with intensely alive brown eyes, thin white graceful hands—a poet and a visionary and a man of action combined. SecState Lowell once called him the ideal Nietzschean man; and he thought of himself in much the same way except that he might have used a different phrase: the adjutant of the new world.

He began by reviewing the history of InterCos and man's eighty-year struggle to reach the stars. He described the hopes, the plans, the tragedies, the effort that preceded the establishment of the first platform, Alpha; and he went on, like a conductor leading a symphony, to the present time. It was a summation of facts that Neil had heard a hundred times before, but he could not help being impressed by Dr. Werner's eloquence. There was no doubt that Dr. Werner considered this the whole reason for his existence. The instruments of a purpose: he, the President of the Council, and the Ministers and their aides, and the entire complex edifice of InterCos subsisted as this only—the instruments of a purpose.

"We have good reason to be proud," he said in conclusion. "We have begun to fulfill the dreams that have haunted mankind for hundreds of generations. On our own planet we have achieved enduring peace. We have accord between all Earth's peoples——" (SecState Lowell smiled) "—we have understanding, prosperity, dignity such as Earth has never known before. We have abolished the multifold madness of war and virtually all weapons of war; we have beaten our swords not into plowshares but into great wings. These wings are straining to go out, out, farther and farther outward, seeking new suns. Alpha, our first platform in space, circles Earth proudly day and night. From Alpha we stepped, as easily as a child steps across a puddle, to Moon. Next, with somewhat greater effort, as a man leaps across a chasm, we sprang to Mars. We shall transform Mars into a garden where millions and millions of our people can live as abundantly as we live here; Mars will be Man's second home in the solar system. But this is only the start of the adventure. Now we are ready to launch our second platform, Beta, which will circle Mars as Alpha circles Earth. And from Beta——"

He paused. He raised his arms and lowered them again. "From Beta," he said slowly, "who can tell where our destiny will lead us? We have overcome the perils, we have learned that we can penetrate the mysteries. The steppingstones outward are being laid one by one. The future of mankind stretches clearly before us amid the stars, and we see that this future is limitless. Our dreams, of which we are the instruments, are ready to be fulfilled. Space, without end—Man's empire."

At Neil's side SecState Lowell stretched his legs and murmured, "*Also sprach Zarathustra.*"

There was a brief interval after the address while the telescreens were lowered all around the Council Chamber. Very politely then, Dr. Werner begged the meeting to teleview the assemblies at the Sahara and Lake Baikal workshops, already positioned on the firing ramps. He showed the reception areas on Alpha, cleared to accept and reassign the assemblies, and the preparations which had been made at New Panama, together with aerial shots of Beta in its almost completed state. The Senior Engineers at the various sites made short statements; and rocket films showed Beta's eventual location relative to the planet itself and its two satellites.

It was a vivid presentation. No further effort of the imagination was required: the touch of a button in Dr. Werner's office, and the final processes in making Beta an effective reality would begin, all this vast machinery would swing into operation. *Our dreams, of which we are the instruments, are ready to be fulfilled—*

Dr. Werner waited a few moments, smiling faintly. He seemed to be saying, "Now you have seen for yourselves. Who would have the temerity to stop this enterprise? Who would dare to stop Beta from taking its place in the Cosmos?" His eyes turned to Crandall, to SecState Lowell, to Neil, as if he were daring any one of them to speak now; and then he said in a loud firm voice, "Before I ask the Council to take action on the time schedule for the Beta Complex there is one other matter which I feel obliged to discuss." He paused and added, "The Ampiti."

He repeated, "The Ampiti," and his lively brown eyes showed amusement. "The Ampiti, or as some of my friends insist on pronouncing the word, the Mpti (like a tribe of primitive African savages) or Ompti or Umpiti." He chuckled. "We have not yet discovered exactly how the word should be pronounced, or even to whom it refers. Nevertheless, I am aware that in recent weeks

17

there has been an increased amount of speculation on this matter." He glanced quickly at Crandall. "It has even been suggested in certain quarters that our entire program should be reconsidered, perhaps halted completely, because of this obscure phenomenon." His eyes moved to Dhevu, to Hsuen, and then to Balatov. "For the record, therefore, it might be well to give a brief description of the Ampiti and their so-called Voices, and what has transpired so far. The Council will then be able to judge for itself whether there is any justification for alarm, or whether the issue may or may not have been raised for political reasons."

Crandall moved angrily; but the President continued to speak, very coldly, very contemptuously.

The facts were simple. These Voices (these so-called Voices) had been heard for the past ten months. They had first been picked up by the old radio telescope at Chamonix, which was being used by research students to check some twentieth-century investigations of radio noise transmissions from Andromeda. Chamonix, puzzled by these unexpected noises which were picked up, sent a tape to the Astro Co-ordinating Committee at InterCos, which sent duplicates to other observatories and asked for reports as a matter of routine. The difficulty at this stage was a shortage of equipment. The old radio telescopes, like the rest of the old radio techniques, had become obsolete many years back, and it was necessary to construct special apparatus to receive the transmissions. When this was done, Hurstmonceux confirmed Chamonix' findings, and so did Mt. Wilson, Hawaii, and Mukden.

Dr. Werner pressed a switch on the desk in front of him. "As an historical curiosity I will play a short section of the original Chamonix tape," and he stood smiling again as the sound poured down from the dome of the Council Chamber.

Neil shivered. The old radio telescopes were crude and unselective, bringing in the whole torrential background of the Universe, the unending scream of the rise

18

and fall of creation from the farthest bounderies of space; they recorded the fury within the whorls of the spiral nebulae, the death throes of solar systems, the wild song of the blue stars. The sounds filling the Chamber were like the sounds in a gigantic foundry, the thunderous mingling of a million processes, the hammers, the shears, the furnaces and the dies of the Creative Force. But except to the specialists there was nothing intelligible in these cracklings, these endless sighs and reverberations. It was merely noise.

And the first recording of the Voices was merely another noise as the Council of Ministers heard it now: a sort of asthmatical wheeze, scarcely distinguishable from the background of static, a vague rustling, a vague and formless stuttering ... *SH* ... *SH* ... *komm* ... *SH* ... *SH* ... *SHSHSHSH* ... *nekomm* ... *Ampiti, ampiti, ampiti* ... *nekomm* ... *NE* ... *NE* ... *SH* ... *SH* ... *nekomm, nekomm, ampiti, nekomm* ... *marzzzh* ... *marzzzh* ... *SH* ... *SH* ... *nekomm* ... *SH* ... *SH* ... *Hhah* ... *Hhah* ... *SH* ... *Hhah* ... *Hhah* ... *Ampiti, ampiti* ... *Hhah* ... *nekomm* ... *Hhah* ...

Dr. Werner turned the recording down. He said drily, "You will have observed that in the Chamonix tape the so-called Voices are very weak. The signal-to-noise ratio, in fact, is scarcely measurable. It was only by accident that the signal was heard at all, so that as a form of communication it is singularly unsuccessful. However, the curiosity of our scientists here at InterCos was quite naturally aroused. Research groups immediately went to work to ascertain what these sounds might be and from where they might be emanating. New, more sensitive apparatus was constructed, and a number of interesting theories were immediately evolved, such as the Johanassen theory that these were reflected echoes of early twentieth-century broadcasts. Doctor Johanassen ignored the obvious fact that even early twentieth-century broadcasts did not produce noises quite as bestial as these."

Dr. Werner looked around, waiting for his words to sink in. The Lord Hsuen laughed delicately.

"In the next six months it was noticed that the signals were growing somewhat stronger," Dr. Werner continued. "They were no more intelligible than before, but they appeared to be more powerful. Because of the repetition of the sound Ampiti (or Ompti) this name was adopted as the code name for the noises; an unfortunate decision, I believe, since it tended to bestow personality on what might well prove to be nothing more than a scientific oddity. This, in turn, led to an extraordinary hypothesis that the noises were an attempt by some unknown agency to get into communication with us; and efforts were made by many scientists and semanticists to translate these peculiar mumblings. In the meantime, receivers had been dispatched and set up on New Panama, and I will play you a recording of the sounds which were heard up there."

The noise came through with much greater force. There was still a disturbing background, static crackling constantly against an incessant rushing sound like a hurricane wind; but the Voices were predominant, shouting out violently and then growing calm and then wailing like hurt children . . . *AG . . . AG . . . agyon . . . agyon . . . agyon, agyon . . . ne ne ne . . . ag . . . ag . . . ne ne ne . . . marzzzh parzzzh ne parzzzh parzzzh parzzzh . . . NE . . . NE . . . k-k-k-kommen . . . ne k-k-k . . . p-p-p-p-p-p . . . AG . . . p-p-p-p-p . . . NE . . . NE . . . ack . ; : ACK . . . AG . . . NE . . . pk-pk-pk . . . k-k-k-kommen . . .*

Then the volume increased, and the fury, the vehemence of the noises made Neil quiver. It was like the sound of animals undergoing painful vivisection, screaming and pleading with the surgeons:

HEE . . . HEE . . . HEE . . . hee ampiti AMPITI . . . hee ampiti AMPITI AMPITI . . . ppp-p-p-p-p . . . nek-k-k-kommen . . . marzzzh . . . hee HEE . . . ne KOMM . . . HUWHUWHU . . . HUW . . . HEE . . . MARZZZH . . . HEE HEE . . . p-p-p-p-p-p . . .

It stopped with a sharp click as Dr. Werner switched it off.

"That," he said curtly, "was the New Panama recording received here a month ago. I must confess that if we are to ascribe those sounds to beings who are consciously attempting to converse with us, then it is hard for me to visualize those beings as anything more than spatial idiots, cosmic lunatics."

The Lord Hsuen laughed again.

Dr. Werner looked around at the Council of Ministers; his gaze finally came to rest on Neil. "These so-called Voices have continued, day and night, for ten months, with only brief periods of silence. Occasionally the transmitting equipment (if we may call it that) appears to break down, sometimes for as long as twenty-four hours —on one occasion for nearly a hundred hours. The source of the transmissions seems to be located about two million miles beyond New Panama, but on this there is no definite agreement: estimates vary and it is possible that the source is not fixed. Recently there has been a further increase in power and reception has been possible on the simplest forms of apparatus, since the transmissions blanket the entire radio spectrum like a modulated X-ray disturbance. On one point our scientists agree: the technical quality is abominable. We could have done better a hundred years ago with the earliest and crudest apparatus. Certainly there is no evidence here of any advanced technology."

His gaze left Neil and then returned. "About the meaning of these unharmonious noises there has been much dispute. I have mentioned Dr. Johanassen's theory, and there have been a hundred more. Perhaps the most interesting is that put forward by the American research group, headed by Dr. Mark Harrison. Dr. Harrison is known to many of us here. He is a scientist of considerable repute. He was responsible for the design of the Beta reactors and worked on them at the Sahara installation during the initial stages. Following an illness which caused his retirement from InterCos he was appointed by his government to head a group investigating extraterrestrial noises. We must consequently listen to him with respect, even though I have yet to be convinced that his qualifications make him an expert on the translation of this Ampiti gibberish. Dr. Harrison suggests that these noises are a warning from the Ampiti to Earth, advising us not to extend our activities beyond Mars. In Dr. Harrison's opinion, the Ampiti have been alarmed by our advances; they have seen us conquering space and will attempt to stop us from going any further. Personally, I am not impressed by Dr. Harrison's theory. I do not see that it has any more validity than the theory of Dr. Johanassen. And in conclusion, I find it inconceivable that such a flimsy hypothesis should in any way affect our plans for Platform Beta. I am sure the Council will agree with me."

Dr. Werner moved his hands gracefully. "That is all I have to say about the Voices of the Ampiti, or Ompiti. I propose that we move to complete the business on our agenda."

He sat down.

Four men sprang up: Prince Dhevu, Balatov, the Lord Hsuen, and Dwight Crandall. Dr. Werner looked benignly from one to another. The dispute between Dhevu and Hsuen was endless, and he had no intention of letting it continue now; he had to choose between Balatov and Crandall, and he decided to dispose of Crandall first. He said, "The Chair recognizes the honorable Minister Plenipotentiary from the United States."

Crandall, big, white-haired, ruddy-faced, said, "Mr. President: in your summation you referred to the work of the American group of scientists investigating extraterrestrial broadcasts. As you pointed out, this group of scientists takes an extremely serious view of the present situation, and I rise on a point of information which I am sure will be of interest to all members of the Council. Would you tell us, sir, whether any steps have been taken to implement the recommendations made by this group, and if so, what has been done so far?" He remained standing, looking at Dr. Werner belligerently.

Neil watched with interest. The elaborate parliamentary language was only camouflage. What Crandall meant, in effect, was, *What the hell is going on here?* And Werner could be expected to reply in equally elaborate and yet equally blunt terms.

The President of the Council said gently, "The honorable Minister is well aware that the group to which he refers was not working within any frame of reference laid down by InterCos. It was not an official group, and while we are always happy to receive reports of the conclusions reached by independent groups InterCos is in no way required to accept such groups' recommendations. I hope that answers the question." He had said, in effect, *Mind your own business.*

"I take it, Mr. President," Crandall insisted, "that the report by the American group has been pigeonholed?"

"No, sir," Dr. Werner answered. "We have naturally been most interested in the report, and our experts have studied it carefully. But as in all such matters, we have relied finally upon the advice of InterCos committees which represent global rather than national interests."

The reply was sharp and malicious.

Crandall reddened. He began angrily, "Mr. President, I object——"

"I believe I have answered your original question, Mr. Crandall."

SecState Lowell whispered, "Take it easy, Dwight," and Crandall sat down. Vernon, the British Minister was standing now, and Dr. Werner said blandly, "The Chair recognizes the honorable Minister Plenipotentiary from the United Kingdom."

Vernon was tall and thin, well-dressed, quiet. "Mr. President, you referred to the suggestion which has been made—not only by the American group of scientists but by some French and British researchers also—that these so-called Voices are attempting to communicate with us, for reasons which are not yet clear. Could you inform us, sir, whether any steps have been taken to establish reciprocal communication from our side?"

Dr. Werner was smiling again. "A memorandum was

circulated two weeks ago to all Delegations describing the steps we have taken. The most important was the reactivating of the old radio station at Leipzig, which is now operating on a round-the-clock basis. In this memorandum all Ministers were invited to participate in broadcasts which would explain and emphasize the peaceful intentions of InterCos, and so far we have put out speeches in basic English, Esperanto, Chinese, Hindustani, Russian, Japanese, German, and even Latin and Greek. We can do little more. Unfortunately, we know of no expert who can speak the utter gibberish which seems to be the language of the Ampiti. So far, the results appear to be negative."

Vernon asked, "Mr. President, can we be sure that these broadcasts can be heard in the space area where the Ampiti appear to be located?"

"We can be sure of nothing," Dr. Werner snapped. "As I said before, we have no evidence that we are dealing with intelligent beings. However, the Leipzig broadcasts are being monitored by New Panama, and in addition we are sending the talks to New Panama by special M-beam relay for rebroadcasting. I say this in order to assure all Ministers that we are doing everything in our power to convey to the Ampiti that Earth will proceed with its interplanetary explorations in a peaceful way." He turned from Vernon abruptly. "The Chair recognizes the honorable Minister Plenipotentiary from the Russian Union."

Balatov, short and stocky, asked in a deep voice, "Mr. President, assuming the possibility that the noises coming to us from outer space may be those of an antagonistic and hostile power, can you inform us what steps are being taken to equip Platform Beta with defenses which would permit it to defend itself against a surprise attack?"

Dr. Werner answered carefully. He said, "I regret that I can give no precise details at this time. Beta's defenses must necessarily remain classified, but I wish to assure the honorable Minister that we have of course taken into account——"

Crandall was on his feet, shouting. "Any heavy armaments on Beta would contravene the Lakehurst Convention, Mr. President. This is serious. If changes have been made in Beta's defenses, the Council of Ministers should have been consulted——"

A bell clanged loudly. Crandall stopped talking, glaring at the President of the Council.

"The chair recognizes the honorable Minister from the Republic of China," Dr. Werner announced in an icy voice.

The Lord Hsuen was standing, frail but singularly impressive in his silken yellow robes. He spoke so softly that Neil could scarcely hear him. "Mr. President, with all due respect, I wish to offer a resolution that this meeting be adjourned for three hours, and the Council of Ministers then reassemble in Secret Executive Session to complete the business of the Chamber."

The Prince Dhevu rose. "Mr. President, I have the honor to second the resolution of the respected Minister."

It was the first time in months that Hsuen and Dhevu had agreed on any matter in a Council meeting.

"Objections?" Dr. Werner demanded, and without waiting he snapped, "So resolved. The session is adjourned."

The bell clanged again, and Crandall turned to SecState Lowell and Neil, and said, "Now we're cooked."

They sat in the Delegation office, Crandall sprawled out in an armchair. SecState Lowell on the corner of a desk, smoking his pipe, and Neil by the door. The sun was just beginning to set, and the pola windows had been adjusted to keep out the glare, but Neil could still see the gleaming surface of the river below, the dimmed rose-red radiance on the horizon. On the right, the avenues were patterned by regular bars of sunlight and shadow, and the Park was a deep, smooth emerald.

"I blew my top," Crandall said moodily. "I acted like a damned fool."

SecState Lowell puffed contentedly at his pipe. He said, "You did what you were supposed to do. You stirred

'em up. Is there evidence that Werner is increasing armaments on Beta?"

"Tell him, Neil," Crandall growled.

Neil said, "We have definite evidence that f-material
is pouring out of the Carlsbad Caverns and Azerbaijan,
and it's going to the two workshops. Stating it in the
most cautious way, we suspect that Dr. Werner is con-
signing it to New Panama."

"Sure he's sending it to New Panama," Crandall cried.
"He's going to have every inch of Beta armed. The Lakehurst Convention expressly forbids the movement of any
f-material, except by specific vote of the Council of Ministers, and that means anywhere—here or in space. It's
completely illegal——"

Lowell said calmly, "Sure, sure. The question is, how
can we stop it? And the next question is, do we want
to stop it? What's your opinion, Dwight? Is Werner
really scared of this Ampiti business?"

"No," Crandall said. "He isn't scared of anything. But
he isn't taking any chances. He sees himself as Superman
and he's going to conquer all space or bust. He doesn't
give a damn for any consequences. The only thing he
can see in front of his eyes is what he described this afternoon—Space without end, Man's empire. What he really
means is, Dr. Werner's empire."

"Can you stall him at this Secret Executive Session
that's coming up this evening?"

"We can try," Crandall said. He sounded bitter. "But
you know, we're outvoted. Vernon and I have agreed, the
only tactics would be to play up this squabble between
Hsuen and Dhevu, and get Balatov involved in it, too,
and anybody else we can drag in. With any luck we can
turn it into an all-night brawl, which will force Werner
to postpone a vote on the Beta time schedule."

"Dwight," SecState Lowell said quietly: "Give me your
own opinion. Is there anything in this Ampiti business?"

"I don't know," Crandall grunted. "We don't have
enough evidence so far." He looked at Neil. "With all
due respect to your brother." He turned back to Lowell,

"Werner may be right. The Ampiti may just be space-idiots fooling around with radio gadgets that they don't know how to operate. On the other hand, Neil's brother may be right, and they may be something serious. That isn't the issue, though. The issue is twofold: shall we let Werner act like a dictator over interplanetary development and exploration, and, secondly, shall we allow Mars to become a dumping ground for surplus populations? Are India and China going to fight over who's to have the lion's share of Mars, with Werner making each of them all sorts of promises, or is the colonization problem going to be settled fairly and squarely?"

Lowell said flatly, "How about you, Neil? What's your feeling about the Ampiti and these Voices?"

"I agree with Dwight, Mr. Secretary. We don't know. There's no definite evidence so far."

"Your brother thinks the evidence is definite enough."

Neil said with a smile, "He's kind of hipped on the subject."

Crandall stood up decisively. "Mr. Secretary, I suggest that you and I have a talk with Vernon and Berkeley. We might have dinner with them.—Neil, there's no reason why you should hang around here. The secret session will go on all night. Take the evening off. You need a break."

"Thanks," Neil said.

"Be sure you have your recall plate with you," Crandall growled. "Just in case of trouble."

Neil patted his breast pocket. "It's here. All ready to buzz."

"If you see your brother," SecState Lowell said, "be sure to give him my regards. Tell him that I'm personally very grateful for the work he's doing and I want him to keep it going, no matter how it's received by Inter-Cos."

"Thank you, sir," Neil said. "Mark will be glad to hear that."

He went to his room in the Delegation suite, and found a message there that Dr. Werner's aide, Hart von

Horstmann, had called him. He put the message aside, took a shower, changed, and then called Hart on the internal teleset. The small screen lit up at once. Hart, blond and handsome, grinned out at him.

"Hi, Neil. I've been calling you for the past hour. How about meeting me for a drink, Neil? I've got the devil of a thirst, boy, I need a drink awful bad. How about it, Neil? Then dinner, maybe. What do you say?"

Hart was always like this, boyish, full of enthusiasm, full of his own particular sort of charm. It was difficult to distrust him, and yet he had to be distrusted.

Neil said, "Sorry, Hart. I have a date."

"Now look, Neil, you wouldn't let me down. Meet me in the lounge, we'll have just a couple of drinks, eh? Then you can go on to your date."

"Next time," Neil said. He switched off the set and went out, took the elevator to the ground floor, marched briskly through the gleaming Arabian corridor to the exit, and signed out there in the Delegation book. The guard said, "Recall plate, Mr. Harrison" and Neil touched his breast pocket again.

"I'll just check it, sir," the guard said. He pressed a button, and the plate buzzed. "That's okay, sir. Good night."

"Good night."

Outside, in the Grand Plaza, the visitors were still wandering around with their children and their dogs, staring at the fountains and the rockets and the great Ad Astra. He strode off toward the car park thinking to himself, "Libby. I'm going to see Libby," and he was a little amused to find that his mind was filled with images of a tall, beautiful and rather puzzling woman. He should have been thinking only of InterCos, of Crandall and Werner, Beta and colonization quotas, Hsuen and Dhevu ... but instead, Libby. He thought, *It must be affection*, and he wondered how it could have happened. The parapsychologists had settled all questions about man-woman relationships long ago. There was sex, which was simple and measurable; and there was affection, which colored

28

sex like the coating on a pill, making it acceptable. Beyond this there was nothing.

It must be affection, Neil thought as he reached the car park, and he laughed to himself. He was whistling as he showed his pass at the booth, and the attendant looked at him in surprise and then smiled.

3

IT TOOK twenty minutes to drive from InterCos to Mark's house in Central Park where he knew he would find Libby, too. There was no way of beating the road feelers. As Neil drove up Fifth Avenue he could hear them, a gentle swish-swish-swish against the speed governor of the little Iranian sports car, sending him on, holding him back at every fourth intersection, keeping him exactly one and a half car lengths from the car in front. The helicopter lanes overhead were just as crowded and just as rigidly controlled. At any given time of the day it seemed as if the entire population of the city was trying to get from one place to another, fifteen million people scurrying around feverishly like ants on an antheap.

The house was surrounded by a high wall, and he was delayed for a few minutes at the gate while he was identified and the three Dobermans were (unnecessarily) called to heel. Many precautions were taken to insure Mark's privacy. The Dobermans, which had been bred by Bavarian specialists, were probably the most effective. They were huge black beasts with claws like those of a mountain lion, and they roamed the grounds looking terrifyingly ferocious. But something had gone wrong in the breeding process, and they were really timid, puzzled creatures who were apt to be scared at the sight of a squirrel. They wagged their stumps of tail at Neil and blinked their sad eyes.

Mark's oldest son, fifteen-year-old Stephen, greeted him

solemnly at the door. He was tall and thin, red-haired, freckled, like the other two boys. They were all destined for scientific careers—Groton, Heidelberg, Cambridge, and M.I.T.

"How do you do, Uncle Neil."

"Hi, Steve."

"Won't you come in, sir?"

"Thank you," Neil said. He was always a little embarrassed by the extreme formality his nephews showed him. Nearly all children were like this nowadays, courteous, thoughtful, studious, well-informed, and joyless. They laughed silently and alarmingly at jokes that Neil could not understand, and they stood in line for hours to see plays like Mjravic's *Poisoner in the Algebraic Madhouse* and Oscar Hammerstein V's *Me and Oedipus.*

"Mother is preparing dinner, sir," Stephen said palely. "Father is below in the workroom." He stood waiting to lead Neil to one or the other.

"Don't worry. I'll find my way."

"Yes, sir. How is InterCos, sir?"

"Fine," Neil said.

"Could you tell me, Uncle Neil, has any detailed report been issued yet on the Martian icosahedrons?"

Neil said blankly, "I don't know, Steve. That isn't my department. I could make inquiries and let you know."

"If you can spare the time, sir. Thank you very much." The boy walked away on tiptoe.

Neil went to the kitchen. Mark's wife, Evelyn, was there, a small bright-faced, New England woman of about forty. With her was Griff Luden, one of Mark's doctors, an apron around his waist, stirring the contents of a large saucepan.

"Neil!" Evelyn cried. She hugged him warmly and stepped back to inspect him. "My goodness, I'm glad to see you! You haven't been here in days. We thought InterCos had swallowed you up."

He said cheerfully, "You're not so wrong, either." He turned to the man. "Hi, Griff. How are things?"

Griff chuckled. "Things could be worse. You're just in

31

time for my special clam chowder, guaranteed to give a wooden Indian ptomaine."

"Splendid," Neil said. He turned back to Evelyn and asked without any emphasis, "How's Mark?"

Her smile wavered. "He's fine, Neil dear. You know."

Neil asked Griff Luden, "Any significant changes?"

"No," Griff replied without looking up. "Nothing special."

Evelyn said, "Why don't you go down and talk to him while Griff and I fix dinner?"

"All right," Neil said.

"Libby's with him. She'll be pleased to see you, too." And Evelyn added as an afterthought, "Poor girl."

Neil said awkwardly, "What's the matter with her?"

"Poor Libby," Evelyn said. "She's been down in the workroom for days helping Mark. She's scarcely been above ground except to go back to her apartment every night. It's a shame."

"Oh," Neil said. He felt uncomfortable.

"You ought to persuade her to relax," Evelyn said. There was a slight twinkle in her eye. "She'll listen to you. I can't do a thing with her. Why don't you take her for a drive after dinner, or to a theater, or something——"

Neil said, "I think you're a scheming female, Evie."

She laughed. "I'm doing my best, Neil."

He left her, feeling unexpectedly irritated. Even though she undoubtedly meant well, his attachment to Libby was personal and private and he resented any interference.

In the hall he took the elevator that went down to the workroom, and even with the doors closed and the elevator mechanism running he could hear the noise below. When he stepped out he was almost stunned by the racket; bursts of sound like prolonged cannon fire bounced off the walls and the ceiling, so loud that his ears seemed to overload and the membranes quivered painfully. At the far end of the room he saw Mark sitting in the big wheel chair, amid the power machines and tables stacked with electrical equipment; and Mark saw him at the same time and waved at him. The noise faded to a hum.

The silence was unnatural for a few moments. Neil heard his own footsteps clanging on the concrete floor as he walked forward, and he fancied that he could hear the pulsing of the blood in his veins. As he reached Mark his voice sounded like a shout. *"Hello."*

Mark said in his thin, high voice, "Glad to see you, Neil. Very glad to see you."

"What the dickens is going on here?" Neil asked. "Are you trying to deafen everybody in New York?"

Mark said, "Tests. That's all. Playbacks. Stuff."

Eighteen months ago he had been like Neil: tall, thin, active. He weighed nearly four hundred pounds now; he was scarcely recognizable for what he had been, and he could scarcely move. His hands were too huge and too misshapen to handle any of the machines in the workroom.

Neil said gently, "What's new?"

"Plenty," Mark said. "Too much." The pasty moonlike face quivered. "You haven't heard?"

Neil sighed inwardly. "The Voices again?" He was bored with the Voices.

"Yes. I tried to reach Dwight Crandall a dozen times this afternoon. Urgent. Had to talk with him. Where's he been, Neil? Where's he been?"

Neil looked away and said casually. "He's kind of busy. You know how it is at InterCos."

The thin voice rose in pitch. "I left a message for Dwight to call me back. Why didn't he do it?"

"I guess he hasn't received your message."

Mark said in sudden fury, "Tell him. Tell him, any time I leave a message it's important. Tell him——" He began to cough and put a hideously white hand over his mouth.

Neil waited.

When the spasm had passed Mark sat breathing heavily. Then he asked in a pathetically weak voice, "Can I reach Dwight now? Tonight?"

33

Neil said in the same careful, casual way, "I don't know. I doubt it."

Mark stared at him for a moment. "Diplomatic, eh," he said, and laughed. "Mustn't talk, eh, mustn't give away little secrets. Good boy." The laugh was an odd titter. "All right. Go and say hello to Libby. You'll find her back there, behind that partition. Don't tell her any secrets, either. Keep everything under wraps."

"Now look, Mark——"

Mark swung the wheel chair around violently.

Neil left him. This was one of the frightful things that had happened to Mark, one of the symptoms of his sickness—sudden flashes of bitterness and violence, for no apparent reason. And yet, Neil thought, you can't blame him. I guess I'd be violent and bitter, too.

He walked between the clustered machines, the lathes and the vertical drill and the presses that Mark could no longer use, and he found Libby sitting at a large steel bench covered with papers and apparatus. Three men were standing behind her, members of Mark's research group. They were all watching the screen of a visual recorder. They did not see him approach, and Neil caught a glimpse of the brilliant-colored picture on the screen. It showed Mark, apparently asleep. The accompanying sound was a painful high-pitched cry.

One of the men turned and said, "Oh, hello, Neil." Libby reached out instantly, and switched the recorder off. She looked round at him, adjusting the red velvet domino over her eyes.

"Neil. How nice to see you." Her voice was friendly, and yet without warmth.

The three men made their excuses and left. Neil said, "I'm sorry. I didn't meant to interrupt——"

"It wasn't anything, Neil."

"You're sure?"

"Sure."

He recalled how he had felt when he was driving from InterCos, the quickening sense of excitement, the increasing sense of affection for her, the desire to be in her presence, to look at her and to listen to the sound of her

34

voice. Now he was in her presence, and the excitement had left him. It always happened. A barrier seemed to rise between them, forcing their bodies and their minds apart, and he could not understand why.

Her smile was cool and observant. He was smiling back at her in the same way, noting the smoothness of her lips and her cheeks, the sparkle of her blue eyes behind the velvet domino, the tied-back ash-blond hair, the long gawky arms and legs that—despite their gawkiness—so often achieved grace. He saw her with the detailed perception of a lover, even though the warmth and affection had dwindled; and he wondered how she saw him.

She said, "You look well, Neil, but a little tired. Have they been working you hard at InterCos?"

"Driving us like slaves."

She half sighed. "Isn't this supposed to be the Age of Leisure? And here we are, all working ourselves to death."

He laughed pleasantly. "Why do it, Libby?"

"Habit," she said. "What else is there to do?"

"All the same," he said, "it seems to suit you. You're pale but——"

She was watching him oddly, and he was unable to finish what he intended to say. She put her hand on his arm. "Let's go upstairs. It must be nearly dinnertime."

There it is again, he thought furiously, that barrier. Is it because of ourselves, the woman she is and the man I am; or is it because of the century we're living in; or is it something that's in the air? Why can't we be simple, and express our feeling simply? Why can't we be alive and affectionate?

He said, "What's this, Libby?"

"What, Neil?"

He was looking down at the recorder on her desk while the thoughts churned in his mind. He said, "This tape."

Her hand twitched as if he had touched some nerve. She said, "Tape?" and glanced down at the recorder and the blank white screen. "This? Oh, nothing. Nothing important, really."

"I caught the end of it. Wasn't it a recording of Mark?"

"An experimental recording." She changed the subject quickly. "You've seen Mark, haven't you? He's told you about the Voices?"

"Oh, Libby, Libby! I'm awfully tired of the Voices."

The way he spoke seemed to offend her; the barrier rose so high that she was unreachable behind it. She said briefly, "Can we go, please? I feel as if I've been cooped up here for a thousand years."

"If you like, I'll take you for a drive after dinner."

Her voice was emotionless. "Thank you."

At dinner everybody laughed a great deal, except Mark's three sons who watched and listened in solemn disapproval. Evelyn was gay and bustling. Griff Luden and the second doctor, Bernard Ismay, told ridiculous stories of their student days in Vienna and Stockholm. The three scientists, not to be outdone, told stories of their student days in Peking, Moscow, Chicago, and Budapest. Mark, struggling clumsily with every mouthful of food, was occasionally ribald. Libby's laughter was cool and light. It seemed a happy dinner party.

And yet it was not. Neil was conscious that all the gaiety, all the brilliant chatter, was hiding—not altogether completely—some underlying disturbance. He saw Ismay's eyes turn sharply several times to look at Mark. He saw Mark suddenly lose awareness of everybody in the room and sit frowning as if some profound problem was troubling him; and then a moment later the bubbly chuckle would come out of him as if he had deliberately put the problem aside. One of the scientists, a big burly man named Jordan Woolley, kept dropping everything that was handed to him, as if he had become afflicted with a nervous disease. Evelyn's vivacity would momentarily leave her, and Neil would see that she was pale and strained, it was an effort for her to maintain her poise. The mask effectively hid Libby's emotions, but he knew that her nerves, too, were strained, in spite of the easy laughter. She kept her face turned away from Mark,

36

but she seeemed aware of every fumbling gesture he made, every pause, every hesitation.

When the coffee was served Mark's patience unexpectedly cracked. He pushed his wheelchair away from the table with such violence that the rubber tires squealed, and said, "I'm going to the study."

The room became silent. Evelyn said, "Would you like to have your coffee served in there?"

He said angrily, "No. No, thanks.—Neil: care to join me?"

Neil stood up slowly. "Sure."

"Libby, you too."

Libby stood up. "Yes, Mark."

"Neil, you can push this damned chariot."

Neil pushed him to the study. It was a big, square room, filled with books and papers, and electronic and M-beam equipment. Near the window there was a desk fitted with a recorder and a control panel, and a couple of electrostatic loud-speakers.

Mark said, ."I want to be near the desk."

Neil wheeled him across the room.

"Thanks," Mark said curtly. "Now sit down, both of you. Make yourselves comfortable."

Libby sat down in an armchair. Neil sat several feet away from her.

"Couldn't you take off that confounded domino?" Mark growled. "I'd like to see your face, Libby."

She said with a smile, "This is my mystery, Mark dear, this is my allure. All the girls are wearing them this year."

"Evelyn doesn't."

"She's a married woman," Libby said, still smiling, "with three children. She doesn't need it."

"Foolishness," Mark said. He hunched forward, brooding over the word. "The world is full of foolishness."

Neil looked at him with pity: a grotesque creature who had been seared and maimed and was waiting to die. The accident had happened eighteen months ago, when Mark was out in the Sahara workshop, supervising the building of the Beta reactors which he had designed. Neil heard

37

later; it was due to sheer carelessness. InterCos was putting terrific pressure on everybody working on Beta
equipment. Dr. Werner was clamoring for his new Platform, his new steppingstone to Man's empire; and despite
the protests of the safety engineers corners were being
cut, elementary precautions were being ignored. It was
a measure of conditions at the Sahara workshop that
Mark's symptoms were not discovered for more than a
week, and by then it was too late to do anything for him.
His kidneys and thyroid had been irremediably damaged
by radiation poisoning.

The ghastly cellular changes began to take place almost as soon as he came back to the United States. He
was given this secluded house in Central Park, Luden
and Ismay were sent from Bethesda to take care of him,
he was presented with everything he wished for—the
power machines with which he could dabble away the
painful hours of leisure, the Dobermans to keep strangers
from intruding on the slow days of dying. When the
Voices were first heard—that scratchy whispering in the
remote darkness of space—he was asked by the Department of Astro-Research to organize the American group
of scientists to investigate the phenomenon and report on
its significance, if any: a kindly thought on the part of
SecState Lowell, really, to make the last months of
Mark's life seem worth while. For a time his brain was
completely unaffected. He retained all his mental powers,
all his brilliance. But lately there had been bad symptoms. Griff Luden had discussed them with Neil a week
ago, coldly and clinically. The flesh was accumulating
too fast, much too fast. And there were signs now that
something was happening to his brain. There were
periods when he had total blackouts, when he became
simply a blind, helpless, unmoving mountain of flesh. A
week ago Griff had given him only another three months
to live.

Neil said mildly, breaking the silence, "What's on your
mind, Mark?"

"InterCos," Mark said.

Libby sat quietly, her head averted from both men.

Neil tried to smile reassuringly. "Now, look. You don't have to worry about InterCos——"

"I am worrying. I *am* worrying. And I'm asking you, what's going on at InterCos right now?"

Neil said, "You know perfectly well I can't discuss my job."

"Sure," Mark said. "You have an oath of office. You've sworn not to divulge any information to unauthorized persons. Failure to observe this oath renders you liable to immediate dismissal from your post, et cetera, et cetera. Right?"

"Right."

"Forget it," Mark said. "This is serious. Libby will tell you. Answer my question. What's going on at InterCos today?"

Neil remained silent.

Mark grinned at him. "Very well, I'll tell you. They're fighting as usual. Hsuen, Dhevu, Crandall, Balatov, Werner. They're fighting over colonization policy, quotas, mineral rights, patrol zones, construction allotments, and all the rest of it. It's a big fight, isn't it? What else?"

Neil met his eyes, and did not answer.

"What else?" Mark cried.

Neil said calmly, "The usual diplomatic conversations. That's all."

"Why can't I get Crandall? Why has SecState Lowell left Washington? It's important that I speak to one or other of them—why can't I reach them?"

"Take it easy, Mark. I'll see that Crandall calls you in the morning."

Mark spread both his swollen hands on the table. "I'm going to ask you point-blank, Neil, and I want a straight answer: is Werner trying to push through the Beta time schedule?"

"You'd better ask Werner."

"Tell me!"

Neil said in a sullen voice, "I don't know."

"You damned fool——"

"Don't fight," Libby interrupted. "Mark, please don't

39

fight. Neil can't talk. You can't force him to talk. Please be reasonable, Mark."

"Thank you," Neil said drily.

She swung round on him. "And as for you, try to understand that Mark isn't doing this for fun. Stop being a diplomatic iceberg."

Mark laughed and closed his eyes. He clasped his hands over his great paunch, as if he were going to sleep. He said in a high childish babble, "You know, kiddies, every now and then I get the impulse to let the world go to hell its own way. This doesn't have anything to do with me. I'm going to hell soon enough——"

"Mark!" Libby snapped.

He opened his eyes and stared at her.

Neil said wretchedly, "I'll tell you this. If it makes you feel any better, Crandall is on your side, and so is Lowell. You needn't have any fears about that."

"I don't care who loves my beautiful blue eyes," Mark shouted. "I want to know what's happening about the Beta time schedule. I want to know if it's going through, and when."

Neil stood up. "Can we talk about something else? Otherwise I'd better go."

"Sit down," Mark growled. "Libby, come here and work the recorder for me."

She walked silently to the desk.

Mark said, watching her hands as she manipulated the controls, "This is an Ampiti recording we picked up this afternoon at Easthampton. We have a big radio telescope there. About three o'clock the chief engineer, Taylor, called me to say we were getting something unusual. He piped it through.—Let it roll, Libby."

There was a bellow from the speakers. She seemed to have trouble adjusting the volume level. Mark laughed wheezily and called across to Neil, "This is the same tape I was playing down in the workroom. Remember?"

Neil nodded. He sat down and leaned back in his chair, once more irritated at having to listen to that wild, unintelligible noise. The room filled with the familiar hiss and the sharp crackle of static; but when the Voices spoke out he stiffened. They were not like the Voices he had heard earlier in the Council Chamber. They blotted out the hiss and the static, they were too loud for comfort, they were clearer, more authoritative. The meaningless syllables were shouted like commands on a parade ground, shaking the room.

AG . . . NE . . . AG . . . NE . . . NO NO NO NO . . . NO MARTA PARTA . . . NO . . . NO . . . NO NO NO . . . NO MARTA PARTA . . . PARZZZA . . . PARZZZA . . . P-P-P-P-P . . . BE . . . BE . . . BE . . . WEEEEEE . . . WEEEEEE . . . BBbroooom . . . BBbroooom . . . BE . . . BE . . . NO NO NO NO . . . .

And then they ceased to shout. They were calmer, restrained, as if they were making a reasoned argument.

NE k-k-kommen, hu-hu. NE k-k-kommen, hu-hu . . . hey-hey, hu-hu . . . paykay paylay . . . paykay paylay kobley kobley, hu-hu . . . Hee Ampiti paylay paykay paylay paykay kobley kobley, hu-hu . . . kobley kobley kobley . . . marzzza parzzza . . . tee tee . . . marta parta . . . marta . . . tee tee . . . marta, hu-hu, hey-hey . . . kobley kobley . . .

Mark touched Libby's arm. She switched the recorder off. He said sardonically to Neil, "Well?"

"Well?" Neil repeated. The noise had alarmed him, and he did not know why.

"It may not have registered with you," Mark said, "but this tape is slightly different from previous tapes." He repeated the word. "Slightly."

"How?"

"Interested?"

"Naturally."

"Imagine that," Mark sneered. "Okay. We can start with the semantics. Libby is our semanticist. Tell him, Libby."

She spoke in a quiet clipped voice, as if she were explaining something in a laboratory. "I have not had an opportunity of studying this tape in as much detail as I should like, but certain features are immediately evident. For example, the clear enunciation of the sound NO. It's repeated several times, each time with the same clarity, and it's very similar to our own way of saying *n-o, no*. It

41

is also used more frequently than the NE sound, which has been predominant in the past. The use of the sound *Marta* is notable, also. I suspect that it's related to the rather mushy *Marzzzh* sound; and, similarly, *Parta* seems related to the old *Parzzzh*. We're getting the T consonant more clearly; but most significant of all, we get sequences of sounds that seem to be equivalent to short declarative sentences."

Mark, smiling, asked, "What about the *BBbroooom BBbroooom* sound? Isn't that new?"

"I think so. I'd have to check back."

"Do you make anything of the *paylay-kobley* stuff?"

"No."

"Do you get an indication of more sense? I mean, it's gabble, but is it less of a gabble than it was?" His eyes were very alive in the dead fleshy face.

"That's what I meant by sequences of sounds," she answered. "They're still not intelligible, but they appear to have a new kind of coherence."

Mark turned to Neil. "I guess our friend Dr. Werner would still call it the gibberish of space idiots, eh?"

"I guess he would."

"What do *you* think?"

"This is way out of my depth, Mark. You're the expert."

"So I am, so I am. All right. You've heard a short report on the semantic or philological aspect of this tape. Now I'll give you an even shorter report on the technical aspect. Did you notice the sound quality of the playback?"

"Yes."

"Clearer, wasn't it? A much better signal-to-noise ratio?"

"If that's what you call it, yes."

"We crosschecked with the monitors on New Panama," Mark said. The smile was fixed on his face, a horrifying grin. "We also crosschecked with the monitors on Platform Alpha. They confirmed our findings. And do you know what?" The grinning face rolled, like the loose head of a grotesque doll.

42

"For God's sake, come to the point," Neil said in exasperation.

"Don't hurry me," Mark cried. "I tried to pass this on to Crandall as soon as I knew. I tried to tell Lowell. I even tried to reach you. I couldn't get past the switchboard operator. You were all too busy with your diplomatic hassles, colonization quotas, patrol zones, who grabs what. So don't hurry me now."

"All right," Neil said. "What's the big news?"

Mark's voice became unnaturally calm. "According to our calculations, the Ampiti are thirty million miles nearer to Earth than they were last night."

Neil stared at him in bewilderment.

"Look, Libby," Mark croaked. "Neil's surprised."

They sat in silence for a while, and Neil tried to understand what Mark meant by this nonsense. It was clearly nonsense. Nothing could move thirty million miles through space in the course of a few hours. Nothing tangible. Nothing that spoke. Nothing that called loudly, NO NO NO NO——

He said vaguely, "We can't reach Crandall tonight. He's in Secret Executive Session. I might try to find Sec-State Lowell. Lowell could get a message passed in to the Chamber——"

"It's too late," Mark said.

"Why?"

"We don't own the only radio telescope in the world. There are thousands of them, all listening to the Voices. InterCos must have heard by now. Their observatories will have picked up the new broadcasts. The question is, what will Werner do?"

"Would you mind if I use your teleset?"

Mark said sourly, "Go ahead."

The Delegation office at InterCos was unsure of Sec-State Lowell's whereabouts. He might be, the operator thought, with Sir Alton Berkeley, in the British Delegation office.

Neil switched to the British Delegation and spoke to the aide there, a man named Stevens. On the screen of

43

the teleset Stevens looked troubled and vague. He confirmed that Lowell and Berkeley were together, but he was under instructions not to disturb them.

Neil asked, "Is the S.E.S. still going on?"

Stevens nodded.

"Has there been any unusual news about the Voices?"

Stevens hesitated.

"Look, Stevens, is that what SecState Lowell and Sir Alton are conferring about?"

"Something of the sort, old chap," Stevens said nervously. "We had a deuced peculiar message from Hurstmonceux."

"If SecState Lowell needs me," Neil said, "tell him to buzz me on recall."

"Right-ho."

"Thanks," Neil said, and switched off.

"Just a few hours too late," Mark said acidly. "Like diplomats all the way back through history."

It still made no sense, movement through space at this rate, thirty million miles in the course of a few hours.

"How could it happen?" Neil asked aloud, looking at Mark. "It's impossible. How could the Voices——?"

Without any warning Mark exploded into a frenzy of rage. "Go away. Damn you, go away. Libby, take him away. Get out of here, both of you. I hate the fools, I hate the fools——"

"Mark!" Libby cried.

"Get out of here, I told you. Get out." He swung his wheel chair around so that he did not have to face them.

Libby said in a low voice, "Come on, Neil," She moved quickly to Neil's side, took his arm and led him out of the study. Bernard Ismay was waiting in the hall, and Libby pushed him gently away from the door to prevent him from entering.

Ismay said suspiciously, "What was all the shouting about?"

She said, "It wasn't anything, Bernie. Something upset him."

44

"He can't afford to be upset," Ismay said angrily. "He's in no condition to be upset. Let me go in there."

"No," she said. "Leave him alone for a minute."

Ismay turned to Neil. "What happened?"

"He lost his temper," Neil said. "Without any reason——"

"He's sick," Ismay said accusingly.

"I know he's sick."

The expression on Ismay's face changed. He said with a helpless sigh, "I'm only a doctor. It's my job to try to keep him alive as long as I can. Griff and I. . . . But what can you do with a man like Mark?—Are you leaving now?"

"Yes," Neil replied.

"I was intending to have a word with you. Okay; let's get it over. Libby, you know already. Somebody in the family should know. We haven't told Evelyn——"

Neil said in alarm, "What's wrong?"

"He's in pretty bad shape, Neil."

Neil said stupidly, "You mean Mark?"

"Yes."

"But Griff Luden told me——"

"Never mind that. We were hoping for three months. His condition has changed for the worse. We think it might be a month now; five weeks if we're lucky."

"You're sure?" Neil said. "You're sure?"

Ismay said, "I'm sorry, Neil. The blackouts are getting more and more serious. The poisoning is spreading faster than we expected. And he's weak. He's been overworking. He needs rest——"

"Bernie," Libby whispered.

Ismay glanced at her, saw her pallor, and said to Neil, "That's how it is. If you want any additional information call me." He shook hands, and without another word went into the study.

"I have to say good night to Evelyn," Neil said.

"Yes. You must."

They went to the dining room and found Evelyn still gay, still vivacious, still the focus of laughter. But when Neil kissed her cheek, tears came to her eyes and she murmured so that only he could hear, "Don't stay away too long, Neil. He hasn't any strength left, he's so dreadfully sick."

"I'll come again soon."

"Thank you, my dear." Then she raised her voice and said brightly, "Have fun, children."

As they walked to the little Iranian sports car Neil said, "I think Evelyn knows."

Libby said, "Of course."

"Weren't Ismay and Luden trying to keep it from her?"

"Yes," Libby said. "But how could they? She loves him."

It was the first time he had heard that word in years. *Love.* A strange, an uncommon, a meaningless word.

The Dobermans barked loudly as they stopped to check out at the gate, then trotted timidly over to the car, sniffed at it and backed away. "Poor beasts," Libby said. "Poor beasts."

Neil nosed the car into the stream of traffic in the Park. He asked in a quiet matter-of-fact voice, "Where would you like me to drive you?"

"Please take me home, Neil."

"You need a break. You need some fresh air——"

"Please," she repeated. "And in any case, I have to go to the apartment to see to Matilda."

Matilda was her pet, a little half-grown poodle.

When they reached the big apartment house on Sixtieth Street he asked, "Shall I wait here? Or shall I go? Or shall I——?"

"I'd love you to come up, if you can bear my company tonight."

He said, "I don't intend to argue with you about that."

She gave him a quick, uneasy smile.

In the apartment she left him for a few minutes; and he sat thinking about her, about her behavior when she was with Mark, about his affection for her, and about how little he knew of her. She was a strange woman, and this apartment itself reflected her strangeness. It was large, airy, chic, with ironwood funiture and brilliant metallic fabrics; there were amusing new flowering plants

46

framed on the walls, scarlet, deep blue, burning yellow, the work of the best bio-artists, and a long tank filled with tropical fish whose metabolism had been slowed down almost to zero so that they seemed to be participating in an exquisitely graceful dance pattern. But with all this brightness and inventiveness it was like a room in one of the ultrasmart Fifth Avenue stores, meant for display, and not to be lived in. He asked himself, *Where is she living now, what is her real habitation? What does she desire, what does she dream about, does affection mean anything to her?*

When she returned he saw that she had changed from her formal day clothes to ruffled pantaloons, a tight-fitting sequined coat, and a black domino. She carried her little dog in her arms, and as she came through the door she whispered in its ear, "Matilda! There's Neil! Go to Neil!" and set it down on the floor.

It scampered joyously and breathlessly across the carpet and tried to jump into his lap. Its legs were not strong enough. Like the Dobermans at Mark's house it was a special breed. The specialists had succeeded in producing only about a dozen of these poodles, jewel-like creatures with coats of pearly scales instead of hair. They were sweet-natured and very intelligent, but a few genetic faults still remained to be overcome: they had no stamina, they were sterile, and they lived for only about a year.

Neil picked the poodle up and stroked it lightly. The scales rustled, and it panted happily at him, showing a blue-red tongue.

"Poor darling," Libby said. "She's been alone all day, locked in my bedroom. She's so pleased to see a human being."

"Shouldn't we take her out for some exercise?"

Libby laughed. "Oh, no."

"Why not?"

"She couldn't walk more than half a block—she'd be exhausted."

Neil touched its ears. It wagged its tail feebly, gave a huge yawn, and lowered its head onto its paws.

"There," Libby said. "You see?" Her voice became slightly sharp. "That's how the latest pet dogs are. You can let them sit like that or you can carry them in your arms, and you don't have any hair coming off on your clothes; and you can keep them for a whole year. Isn't that marvelous?"

He made no comment.

She went on, with the same sharpness, "The only drawback is that you're apt to become fond of the creatures, you become attached to them, and then you wonder why——" She stopped, biting her lower lip.

"Come and sit down, Libby."

She sat down beside him silently, her legs outstretched, her head tilted back against the bar of the settee.

"You must be very tired."

She considered his statement for a moment, and turned her head and smiled at him. "Tired? No. Not really. I'm just being adolescent, I guess, wondering why things like this have to be. Matilda. And Mark——"

"There's nothing we can do about Mark."

"I know."

"It's tragic and terrible, but we have to accept it."

"I know, Neil. I know."

"Everything that *could* be done *was* done for him. You're upset and hurt, Libby. So am I. The only consolation we have is that he's had the best possible care, and comfortable surroundings, and work that's occupied him every minute of his time."

She said bitterly, "You sound so smug," and turned her head away, looking at the slow-moving fish in their illuminated tank.

The words hurt him. "That isn't true. I'm not smug about Mark. I respect him and admire him——"

"You've done everything except listen to him."

"That isn't true either——"

"Yes," she said. "That's why he drove you out tonight. He couldn't take that smugness any longer. All the double talk, all the evasion——"

"You were there," Neil said angrily. "You saw me go to the teleset and try to reach SecState Lowell."

48

"Of course," she mocked. "You had an awkward fact thrown at you. The Ampiti are thirty million miles nearer than they were last night. And what did you do? You tried to inform your superior officers at InterCos."

He said, 'You're tired and you're being unreasonable."

"Neil. I'm not tired. I just feel the same way Mark did. I feel sick and wretched and hopeless. None of you really believe in Mark's work. You only think about how you can use it to your own advantage, against Werner, against Hsuen and Balatov and the others. We've done our best to convince you but you won't be convinced, and now let the world go to hell its own way, as Mark said."

The little poodle stirred on Neil's lap, and gave a tiny bark.

She cried quickly, "Oh no, Matilda, I'm not angry with you, poor dear. I'm very fond of you, you know that."

Neil said, "Would it be possible for you to repeat those words to me?"

She reached for his hand. "Yes. With a little effort, but yes, if it matters to you."

"It matters a great deal."

She said with a weak sigh, "I'm very fond of you, Neil, very fond; but everything is such an awful mess."

"Is it?"

She smiled. "I guess I am a product of my age. Like the Ampiti." The simile made her laugh.

He waited a few moments before asking, "Would you care to tell me exactly what's on your mind?"

"I doubt that you'd enjoy hearing it."

"Try."

She said, "There's a lot on my mind, but some of it is very personal and I could only tell it to a parapsychologist, and I have a suspicion that *he* would go into a screaming fit if he heard it; so would you mind if I skipped that part?"

He waited.

"But some of it is fit for public consumption, Neil dear, and if you care to listen——"

49

"Yes. Go ahead."

"Very well." She drew away from him, her body stiffening as she began to talk. Her voice was cold and precise as it had been earlier. "Mark is on my mind. Mark is terribly on my mind. InterCos, of which you are a part, of which Crandall and Hsuen and Dhevu and Balatov and Dr. Werner are a part, has chosen to ignore Mark's reports——"

"No!" Neil cried.

"Except," she continued, "where they can be used as a basis for political maneuvering. Mark has made certain definite recommendations in his reports. One is that all work on the Beta Complex should immediately be stopped. Crandall agrees with this. Why? Not for the reasons Mark has advanced, but because it would damage Werner's prestige, it would give more time for a possible deal with Dhevu, and it would enable the question of colonization quotas to be reopened. Those aren't Mark's reasons."

"We know Mark's reasons," Neil said. "He's scared of the Ampiti. But our reasons are more practical. We want a fair apportionment of Mars, and we want that principle understood and accepted before Werner sets off on any more conquests."

"The critical word is conquests," Libby said. "Look at that pretty word. Say it to yourself. Roll it around your tongue a few times." She laughed. "And I thought it had gone out of fashion. Like slavery, and war, and all those wicked things we used to read about in history books."

"You know what I mean," Neil said.

"Of course I know what you mean," she said, and laughed again. "You mean conquests. You mean the conquest of Mars, and the conquest of any other solid objects in space that will provide loot in one form or another.—Am I being very cynical, Neil? Shall I go on?"

"Please go on."

She said, rather thoughtfully, "We had quite a day today. We were kept quite busy. For example, there was that visual tape which we were looking at when you

50

arrived. Mark had one of his bad blackouts, as usual; but he had asked us beforehand to tape it because of some theory that during these blackouts he might conceivably make some sort of extrasensory contact with the Ampiti——"

"That's fantastic," Neil said angrily.

"Not so very fantastic," Libby said. "Something must happen during those blackouts. As it turned out, we couldn't find any evidence of the kind Mark hoped for. —And then, earlier in the afternoon, Mark, Jordan Woolley and I held an hour's conference, and Mark dictated a new report to Crandall. As you know, Mark tried to reach Crandall this afternoon but couldn't. So he put what he had to say in the form of a report which he sent over to the Delegation office. But I daresay Crandall won't read it until morning—if at all."

"Crandall will read it," Neil said.

"That's splendid," she said tartly. "I only hope it doesn't have the same effect on him that it had on Jordan. Did you notice how Jordan dropped things all during dinner? He couldn't even hold his knife and fork in his hands. To be perfectly honest, I felt rather the same way myself."

Neil asked, "What's so alarming about this report?"

"You must borrow it from its pigeonhole when you have some free time."

He said, "Libby, don't speak to me like that. Tell me."

She was silent.

He repeated, "Tell me."

"All right. If you're really interested." For one moment she looked pathetically tired, and his heart went out to her in anxiety, but she immediately recovered her poise.

She said, "Mark simply asked some questions, and guessed at the answers. For example, assuming our calculations were correct, how was this thirty-million-mile leap accomplished by the Ampiti in a few hours? . . . Answer: we don't know. We can only assume that the Ampiti have more advanced methods of space transportation than InterCos, or that they have a number of

Platforms which are being utilized in leapfrog fashion. If this latter assumption is correct, they may be in process of making yet another leap nearer Earth."

"Go on."

"Secondly, how can we envisage such techniques being used by beings who are so poorly equipped in the means of communication? After all, they only gabble and talk gibberish, don't they? Answer: it is possible that the Ampiti do not normally communicate as we do, that speech is unknown to them and that in the development of their means of communication they by-passed radio. Thus they may have been forced to go to great pains to discover how radio works, to evolve the thermionic tube which even we have now discarded, and so on. However, it must be noted that on the new platform they seem to have improved their equipment and it is probably provided with a new kind of transmitter and new speech-making apparatus."

Neil was startled. "Speech-making apparatus?"

"Yes. Why not?—Thirdly, can we extract any meaning from the sounds we are receiving? Answer: only to a limited extent. These sounds may have been a way of saying, 'Hello, hello,' or 'We are waiting to see your shining faces, dear brothers,' or as the American group has maintained, they are a warning to us not to come too far out in space. The key words have always been *ne* and *kommen*. They seem obvious—a simple French word combined with a simple German word to mean *Don't come*. But they might be accidental. The whippoorwill doesn't say the words *whip-poor-will*, but it pleases us to think that it does. Similarly with *ne kommen*. However, the apparatus on the new platform clearly says something that sounds precisely like *NO*; it still says *ne*, but it says *NO* with greater emphasis, and it also says with equal emphasis *MARTA*, and *PARTA. No Mars parta.* The meaning, Mark suggests, is *Do not pass Mars*."

Neil reached out and took hold of her hand. She made no sign that she felt his touch. He said, "Go on, please."

"Fourthly, a whole new series of sounds has now appeared. *Paykay kobley*, and so on. In particular, the heavily accented word *BBbroooom*. Is there any significance in this? Answer, again we can only make a guess. The tone of the sounds varies from a sort of cajolement to a sort of threat. The heavy sound *BBbroooom*—used as a threat—is fairly obvious: a deep and explosive noise."

She paused at this point.

"Is that all?"

"Yes, except for Mark's final paragraph. This is how he concluded: 'The American group believes on the basis of its first examination of the new transmissions that the Ampiti are alarmed by our space activities, that they are demanding that we shall not extend these activities beyond Mars, and that this demand is now being accompanied by a threat of war.' Mark signed it, Jordan Woolley signed it, and I signed it."

Neil sat back thoughtfully. He shook his head. "No, Libby. Even Crandall is going to find that rather flimsy."

She said, "I suppose he will," and released herself carefully from his hold and stood up. She smiled down at him and murmured, "Look how peacefully Matilda is sleeping on your lap," saying the words as if everything else she had said in the last few minutes was of no greater importance.

She walked slowly to the window and looked at the street below, and he could see that she was disturbed. He felt a new stirring of affection for her, and he put the little poodle gently on the settee and went across the room to join her.

He said, "Could we talk about something else now?"

She did not reply.

He went on, "The Ampiti are still hundreds of millions of miles away. We still don't know anything that's really positive about them. We're just frightening ourselves, it seems to me, like children——"

She swung round unhappily. "Oh, Neil! Neil, don't say that."

He said, "I wanted to talk to you about other things tonight. As I came to Mark's house, I was thinking——"

53

The recall plate buzzed in his breast pocket, interrupting the words he was going to say.

She stood looking at him. "Yes?"

He said, "I've never ignored a recall signal before, but this is one I didn't hear because I have something to say to you. I want to ask you, Libby——" But he had no opportunity to go on. The recall plate buzzed again, three times, an emergency recall; and he said, "I'm sorry. I can't ignore that. I have to leave right away. Shall I see you tomorrow?"

She answered distantly, "I hope so."

He took her in his arms and kissed her. For a moment she clung to him and he could feel her body trembling with agitation; then she released herself and said, "You must hurry. They're waiting for you at InterCos," and walked with him to the door of the apartment.

4

CRANDALL'S office was crowded. The three English-
men were present, Sir Alton Berkeley, Geoffrey Vernon,
and Stevens; and also McAllister, the Canadian Minister;
Waterson of Australia; Locke of New Zealand, and their
three aides. As Neil entered Crandall strode over to him
and said in a low growl, "Sorry to recall you like this.
SecState Lowell thought you ought to sit in.—Did you
see your brother this evening?"

"Yes."

"Have you heard this new stuff about the Ampiti?"

Neil nodded.

"Is Mark taking it very seriously?"

"Yes," Neil said.

Crandall said noncommittally, "H'm," and walked
back to his place. SecState Lowell stood up and tapped
gently on Crandall's desk with the bowl of his pipe, and
the room became quiet.

Lowell said, "In the past few hours there have been
certain developments which concern us all, on which
we should all be fully informed, and which call for the
frankest discussion. Those are the reasons for calling this
private meeting. The transcriber will go to Code Blue."

Crandall twisted a dial on his desk, locking the doors
of the office and the anterooms, and putting the automatic recording apparatus into cipher.

"Dwight," Lowell said. "suppose you start the ball
rolling."

Crandall spoke gruffly, giving a brief description of the events at the secret session. It was like a description of a fencing match: lunge and riposte, maneuver and countermaneuver, subtle and deadly.

Werner had opened the meeting with another harangue about the urgency of approving the Beta time schedule, and had asked for an immediate vote.

Vernon had stalled him very neatly at once by raising the question of the dispute between Russia and Australia concerning patrol craft. The final sections of Beta, Vernon had pointed out with faultless logic, would require a convoy during transit. A decision would have to be made beforehand which craft would be used on the convoy, which would make up the advance- and rear-guard patrols, and so on. But this decision couldn't be made until the Russo-Austral dispute was settled; and Vernon had justifiably insisted that the matter would have to be thrashed out by the Council of Ministers before there could be any approval of the time schedule.

Balatov had answered, surprising everybody by stating mildly that he was fully prepared to accept the *status quo,* and that in the interests of global unity he would withdraw his protest about the Australian patrols violating Russian zones.

Waterson had immediately jumped up with a rebuff. He refused, without qualification, to accept Balatov's proposal. The Australian government, he stated, wanted the matter discussed in detail, and a full apology from the Russian government.

Every effort had been made to keep this argument going. Locke, the New Zealander, had joined in; so had McAllister. So had the Polish and Hungarian Ministers, speaking for the other side. But finally Balatov had intervened with the unprecedented statement that he believed an apology from the Russian government would be forthcoming; and Hsuen, thereupon, asked the Council to vote on whether the dispute should be discussed at this session or settled privately and amicably.

The vote had gone in favor of Balatov. Rather alarmingly, Dhevu had voted with the pro-Werner bloc.

Crandall's voice was gloomy as he continued. "Next we raised the question of colonization quotas. Locke made the argument that the Council of Ministers was hopelessly split on this issue and that all further space projects must of necessity be held in abeyance until a satisfactory agreement was reached. He pointed out that the quotas were heavily loaded in favor of the Chinese, and that the Indians—with a much more serious problem of overpopulation—had been allotted a ridiculously small quota.

"Hsuen answered. He said that his government had given this question very serious consideration and had come to the conclusion that the Indians had been most unfairly treated. His government, therefore, was prepared to make considerable sacrifices; and he proposed an entirely new method of apportioning the quota percentages which would be greatly to India's advantage— that is, on the basis of national birth rates, present and estimated."

Crandall looked around the room and smiled wryly. "I think you all know where that would leave us. We should be out in the cold as far as the development of resources on Mars is concerned. Dhevu, of course, immediately said he was grateful for the new spirit the honorable Chinese Minister had brought to the question, and he was fully prepared to enter into new quota discussions. He saw no reason why the Beta project should be delayed while these were taking place, however. Balatov suggested a vote. As before, the three blocs voted together. We were defeated.

"At this stage, I need hardly say, we were in a hopeless position. Werner was now ready to push forward the vote on the Beta time schedule. It was then that he received a triple-Red signal from his aide, Hart von Horstmann, indicating news of such importance that a Secret Executive Session could be interrupted. This was the message, confirmed by several observatories, that the Voices of the Ampiti had apparently moved forward some twenty-five to thirty million miles. Werner was obliged to pass this information on to the meeting; and I guess I can say we were saved by the bell, or rather by a bombshell. Balatov began to lecture Werner about Beta's defenses, and then Dhevu rose and asked for an immediate adjournment so that this new development could be studied. He seemed very alarmed. McAllister promptly seconded him. In the general excitement we were also able to ensure that the meeting, when it reconvenes tomorrow morning at ten o'clock, will be an Extraordinary General Session—which means that the issues can be discussed out in the open; so the battle is not yet lost."

Crandall sat down.

SecState Lowell asked, "Any comments?"

Berkeley said in his beautifully modulated voice, "It seems from Mr. Crandall's excellent summary that two points arise. First, Hsuen, Dhevu, and Balatov had evidently come to an agreement to support the program of Dr. Werner, and I have no doubt that they have been promised concessions in return which are capable of doing us great harm. Secondly, this alliance was most providentially disturbed by these reports concerning the Ampiti; and with commendable promptness our representatives on the Council of Ministers exploited this situation to obtain a welcome delay at a most critical moment. What we now have to consider, I think, is how this situation can be still further exploited to our advantage."

Spoken in that low smooth voice, the phrase still jarred on Neil's nerves: *exploited to our advantage.*

"I must confess," SecState Lowell said in his best diplomatic manner, "that I am rather puzzled by the news about the Ampiti. How was it possible for these noises to move some thirty million miles through space overnight?"

"I've just had a word about it with one of our fellows in London," Berkeley said, beaming at Lowell. "Quite simple, really. He told me it's nothing but refraction, or reflection—which is it, Stevens?"

"Refraction, sir," Stevens said promptly.

"Refraction," Berkeley repeated. "Caused by a cloud of space dust, or something. Lots of clouds up there, I understand, accumulations of dust. Very untidy. However, that's the cause. Sort of a mirage, you know. Very lucky for us, but nothing to get excited about."

SecState Lowell said, "That sounds like a good theory. Anybody else?" He asked a little more loudly, "Does anybody here feel that we should discuss this phenomenon *apart* from its effect upon the present situation; or, in other words, that the advance of the Ampiti (if it is such) might constitute a threat in itself to our terrestrial security?"

"I don't like it at all," Vernon said quietly.

Berkeley turned to look at him in amused surprise.

"I listened to a playback for a few minutes before I came to this meeting," Vernon continued. "I found the experience definitely alarming. I believe we should be extremely careful. I believe it is possible that we are facing an unusually grave threat."

Berkeley said reproachfully, "Really, my dear chap! I can understand Dhevu showing alarm, but I didn't expect it from you."

Vernon said, "SecState Lowell asked for opinions. I merely stated mine."

SecState Lowell said, "Dwight, could we have Mark Harrison's report?"

Crandall stood up again. "Dr. Harrison was in possession of this news about the Ampiti early in the afternoon, and I understand made several attempts to reach us. Unfortunately he was unable to do so because I'd given instructions that we were not to be disturbed during these critical sessions." He smiled. "Otherwise we might have been able to throw this bombshell into the secret session ourselves."

He picked a folder off his desk. "Dr. Harrison appears to be very worried about this new business, even more than Vernon is. I have here a report, prepared in great haste by Dr. Harrison and signed by two other members of the American group, Dr. Jordan Woolley and Dr. Elizabeth Hewes; and with your permission I should like to read it, since it might prove of valuable assistance in deciding our strategy tomorrow."

Strategy! Neil thought. *Strategy!*

And then he thought, *Of course. That's what we are considering. Strategy. How to outwit Balatov, Hsuen, Werner, and the others. I mustn't be naive about this. The word is strategy, to discover what we can exploit to our advantage.*

"Go ahead, Dwight," SecState Lowell said.

The report was substantially the same as that which Neil had heard earlier. It included some complex mathematical data and a more detailed semantic examination of the new words and the new phraseology which the report claimed was so signfiicant in the latest broadcast. *This is important,* Neil found himself thinking: *this is after all very important,* and he watched the other men in the room for their reactions. SecState Lowell and Vernon were grave and attentive. Berkeley and Stevens were smiling. McAllister was bored. Locke was puzzled. Waterson, also puzzled, was sitting forward as if he were trying to catch one phrase that might clarify the whole matter for him.

Crandall paused before he reached the end of the document. He said, "I now come to Dr. Harrison's final recommendations," and glanced at SecState Lowell significantly before he resumed reading. "I quote: 'If this analysis is correct, and even if some of the foregoing deductions are at fault, it is obvious that InterCos must now exercise the utmost caution, and should wait for further developments before proceeding with any new projects. All work relating to the Beta Complex should be halted, at least temporarily, both at the Sahara and Lake Baikal workshops, and on Platform Alpha and at New Panama. The American group believes on the basis of its first examination of the new transmissions that the Ampiti are alarmed by our space activities, and that they are demanding that we shall not extend these activities beyond Mars, and that this demand is now being accompanied by a threat of war.'" Crandall closed the folder, saying, "That's all." He sat down.

Berkeley pulled a large silk handkerchief out of his pocket and loudly blew his nose.

"Sir Alton?" SecState Lowell said.

Berkeley carefully rearranged the handkerchief in his pocket. He tried to look solemn, but a trace of his smile remained. "Are we supposed to take this seriously, Mr. Secretary? Greatly to my regret, I find myself unimpressed."

Waterson said bluntly, "I'm not impressed, either. It sounds to me like a lot of highfaluting balderdash."

"I should hate to appear an ally of Dr. Werner," Berkeley said, his voice hardening, "but let us be clear on this matter. We are all opposed to Werner's philosophy and his opportunist methods, which are without any doubt capable of doing us considerable harm. However, he is no fool. His reaction to Dr. Harrison's report would be decisive and forthright—like our good friend Waterson's—and I feel sure he would carry the majority of the Council of Ministers with him. He would assail the report, as I do, for being alarmist without any foundation. He would ask, as I do, where is the positive evidence that the new broadcasts are a threat? He would produce the evidence of equally reputable scientists to demonstrate that the so-called movement of these Voices is simply an illusion, a freakish natural phenomenon. And finally he would ask, again as I do, if these broadcasts are indeed a threat then *who* are the Ampiti, *where* are the Ampiti, and with what do they threaten us? What forces do they have at their disposal, and what weapons have they at their command? And are we to run away, are we to abandon all space exploration every time we hear a whimpering noise in the night? Mr. Secretary, I am still heartily opposed to Dr. Werner, but I fear that on these issues I should not be able to put up any worth-while argument."

Locke said, "Sir Alton, don't you think this report still

61

provides us with a chance to block Werner by indirect means?"

"No, Mr. Locke," Berkeley said stiffly. "But I should be glad to hear your suggestions."

"For one thing, there's the important factor of public opinion. If the new broadcasts are interpreted as a threat to our terrestrial security there would be widespread alarm—probably enough to make Werner back down for the present."

Berkeley said with a gleam of interest, "You're suggesting that we arouse public alarm by issuing this report?"

SecState Lowell said, "I'm afraid that's impossible. The report is secret. We couldn't issue it without authorization from the Council of Ministers."

"We could get round that," McAllister said. "We could pass the word to the news and telepic agencies. Suggest that Dr. Harrison has a good story. Arrange for him to hold a press conference. That ought to turn the trick."

SecState Lowell said, "I'm sorry. I couldn't agree to that policy. It could be extremely dangerous. It would only serve to undermine public confidence in InterCos, and it might have the most serious future consequences. We can't cut off our nose to spite our face. And in any case, we don't have time for byplay of that sort. We're trying to decide on a line to follow at the meeting tomorrow morning.—Mr. Vernon?"

Vernon spoke slowly and reluctantly. "Mr. Secretary, I'm still concerned about this new situation. It seems to hold many dangers. But, as you point out, we are trying to decide on our tactics tomorrow morning. In that connection I should like to draw attention again to the fact that our principal objective is to gain the support of the Dhevu group. It was very noticeable that Dhevu was greatly disturbed by Werner's announcement tonight, and I think we should try to exploit this aspect of the case."

"That makes sense," Crandall said.

62

Berkeley snapped, "How do you propose to exploit it?"

"Frankly," Vernon said, "the report I just heard only increased my misgivings. Very well, I suggest it might have the same effect on Dhevu. Let's try the effect of exposing Dhevu to Dr. Harrison's theories."

"What do you mean by *expose?*" Berkeley demanded.

"I propose that when the session convenes in the morning we put forward a motion that Dr. Harrison be invited to address the Council of Ministers."

Neil said quickly, "Sir, he's very sick. I doubt if he could make it."

"We can send an ambulance for him, if necessary," Vernon said. "Or he can make his statement by M-beam. It doesn't matter. The important thing is for Dhevu to have an opportunity of hearing Dr. Harrison directly." He smiled in an odd, abstracted way.

"Comments?" SecState Lowell asked.

Locke said, "I'm for it. Even if Werner throws the motion out, it might only serve to make Dhevu more nervous."

Crandall said judiciously, "Yes. It's a good idea."

Berkeley said in a morose voice, "I think the idea has certain merits. It does not commit us in any way. It throws all responsibility on an expert."

McAllister and Waterson agreed, and the plan was then worked out in detail. Vernon would propose the motion as soon as the meeting opened in the morning, after a brief résumé of the report and its implications. Beforehand, SecState Lowell would use his influence with one of the Scandinavian delegates to second the motion. Crandall would confer with Mark Harrison, and arrange for him to prepare a statement that could be read to the Council. In the meantime, a copy of the report would be sent confidentially to Dhevu for study.

"Is that all?" Berkeley said, yawning. "Because, honestly, I'm ready for bed."

"I guess that's all," SecState Lowell smiled.

Crandall turned the dial on his desk, unlocking the doors and releasing the automatic recording apparatus and communications equipment. At once the bell on his teleset rang three times—Priority Red—and the signal was repeated until he answered it.

He said, "It's for you, Mr. Secretary. Dr. Werner."

The room immediately became quiet. Lowell went to the teleset, listened, and answered in a subdued voice. Then he switched the teleset off and looked at Berkeley with a subdued grin. "The good Doctor has been trying to reach us for the past twenty minutes. He asks if you and I would kindly step up to his office for a few moments, on a matter of the greatest importance. Now, what the dickens does that mean?"

McAllister said, "Shall we wait here?"

Lowell said, "Somebody ought to get some sleep, even if Berkeley and I don't. We'll let you know if it's really as important as Werner thinks."

Locke said, "To tell you the truth, I'd be glad of a good night's sleep. I'm getting tired of the Ampiti and Dr. Werner. They give me nightmares."

Berkeley grunted.

Once again, returning to his room in the Delegation suite, Neil found a message that Hart von Horstmann had called him. By InterCos rules the call had to be returned as soon as possible.

After the long discussion in Crandall's office he felt tired. It was really more than physical fatigue. The relentless maneuvering had disturbed him, the ingenious planning of clever men intent on outwitting other groups of clever men, the tacit assumption that any means were permissible to achieve a certain end. *Sure,* he thought bitterly, *sure, we have to beat Werner. But is this the only way to do it? Bringing in a sick, a dying man to make a grandstand play?*

Politics, he thought, *politics.*

And now here was Hart von Horstmann waiting to indulge in another maneuver in this unrelenting political game. On behalf of Werner, of course, hoping to pick up a few crumbs of information about what had been decided at Lowell's private meeting. Hart von Horstmann, Dr. Werner's blond, good-looking, affable young vulture.

He made the call on the internal teleset. Hart, smiling his unalterable smile, said, "Hi there, Neil. How's the boy?"

"Hello, Hart. What's on your mind?"

"How about meeting me for a drink, eh, Neil? You must be awful thirsty after the long conference you just finished. How about meeting me down in the lounge?"

Neil said, "It's one-thirty, Hart. I'm tired."

"I'm tired too, boy. My bones are creaking, listen." The smile remained fixed, but his eyes seemed to change, they seemed to become urgent and appealing. "Just one drink, that's all. A nightcap, Neil."

"I don't need a nightcap. Thanks all the same."

"It's about your brother," Hart said, and his smile faded momentarily and then reappeared. "The lounge, eh? In a couple of minutes?"

More politics, Neil thought. *Now Werner's using my brother. And I guess I have to find out how and why and wherefore. It's my duty to find out.*

He said sourly, "All right," and switched off.

Hart was waiting for him in the lounge on the twenty-fifth floor, sitting in a shadowed corner by one of the great windows that looked across the East River. The wild currents of Hell Gate whipped the water into phosphorescence below; beyond were the lights of Long Island and the accumulating darkness of the Atlantic Ocean.

"Hi," Hart said, "good old Neil." Even in the shadows he looked golden; bronzed, clean, very handsome, without any signs of fatigue. Neil had the impression that he must have been a genius at some strenuous sport— tennis, or discus throwing, or diving. He had the litheness, the graceful power that the Greeks loved and immortalized.

"Hello," Neil said coldly.

Hart laughed. "What will you have to drink, Neil. Eh?"

65

"Skip the drink. Tell me what's worrying you about my brother."

"Relax," Hart said. He spoke into the table microphone. "Two brandies, please." He switched the microphone off, and kept his thumb on the switch. "You don't need to drink. Just make-believe. That's not too difficult, is it?"

"Make-believe. Why? What's the idea?"

"There are other people in the lounge. They may be watching us. Neil, we're just two gay young fellows dissipating after a hard day's work, you see?"

"I don't see. I'm not dissipating. I'm tired and I want to get to bed. Now, what about my brother?"

The brandies arrived on the service belt beside the table. Hart took them and placed them elaborately on the table. "The rule is to warm the glass between the hands for several minutes to release the bouquet, as you are aware.—I admire your brother greatly, Neil. I was thinking about him today. I should very much like to meet him."

"He's too sick," Neil said. "I'm sorry. The doctors won't permit him to have visitors."

Hart said, "Oh." He turned the glass slowly in his hands. Then he said with great seriousness, "Have you heard of Dr. Wolfgang Rebling, a German doctor?"

"No."

"He has been doing interesting work on radiation poisoning. He claims to have developed a new system of treatment."

"It's too late," Neil said.

"I don't understand what the treatment really is. I believe Rebling uses certain metals like a poultice. He claims the metals will absorb the radiation."

"That sounds pretty phony," Neil said. "But anyway, it's too late."

"You're sure? Because it wouldn't be too difficult to have this man flown over for special consultation. It could be arranged immediately."

"No," Neil said. He felt the sour gall flow into his

66

mouth. "No. His personal doctor told me tonight that he can only live for about a month. Thanks for the interest."

"Then the system is damaged beyond repair? Too bad. He's a great man, Neil. I'm terribly sorry."

Tricks, Neil thought, *tricks, very subtle tricks. Why? Is he trying to win me away from my Delegation?*

Hart looked at Neil, and looked down again immediately. "You may be interested to know—you will hear soon enough—that Dr. Werner has received new reports in the past hour from New Panama and Platform Alpha. He has decided to inform all important dignitaries first, such as Madame Ai-Wen-Tai, SecState Lowell, Sir Alton Berkeley, and so on, since they are all key members of their respective governments; and he will probably inform Ministers afterward."

"Inform them of what?"

Hart said quietly, "New Panama has reported five unidentified objects flying at twenty thousand miles west of the observatory."

Neil said, in shock, "No!"

Hart continued, "What is more remarkable, we have a similar report from Platform Alpha. Five unidentified objects, one thousand miles overhead." He glanced sideways out of the window. "Which, as you are aware, places them only six thousand miles from where we are sitting.—Drink your brandy, Neil."

"It's impossible."

"Yes. Utterly impossible. Of course."

Neil stared at him.

Hart said in the same quiet voice, "Your brother will be interested, don't you think?"

"If this is true I'll have to get back to my Delegation fast."

"It's true," Hart said. His voice became lighter, amused. "Why worry? You have your recall plate? They'll buzz you as soon as they need you."

"You're sure it isn't a rumor? Somebody's idea of a joke?"

"I assure you," Hart said. "I assure you, it's true.—
Tell me: is it really too late for Dr. Rebling to examine
your brother? Why don't we try, why don't we take a
chance?"

"You should have thought of it eighteen months ago."

"I guess so, Neil—the poor guy. You know what? I
have a great personal desire to have him live on, to
to have him live on a lot longer."

"You have?" Neil said thinly.

"Yes. Partly for the good reason that I should like to
live on a few years longer myself." He grinned and
brushed his blond hair back in a nervous gesture. "I'm
feeling melancholy, my dear fellow. A little spooky. I
don't like to be overlooked, even from so many thousands of miles. Drink up. I'll order another one, so we
can enjoy ourselves and also be in good spirits for the
next conference——"

The recall plate buzzed in Neil's pocket. He looked
at his untouched glass, hesitated, and then stood up.
He said, "I'll be seeing you, Hart, thanks for the drink,"
and walked away.

SecState Lowell was alone in Crandall's office, sitting
as he often did on the edge of Crandall's desk, smoking
a pipe. He waved a long arm at Neil and said, "Come
in, come in. Keep me company."

"Yes, Mr. Secretary."

"Sit down. No need to be formal."

"Thank you," Neil said. He leaned against an arm
of one of the conference chairs.

"Dwight's up with Werner," Lowell said dreamily.
"All the Ministers have been called in for a special announcement from our Nietzschean friend."

"Unidentified objects?" Neil said.

Lowell glanced at him in surprise.

"Hart von Horstmann just told me the news," Neil
explained.

"Is that so? Since when does that young man discuss
confidential information with members of other delegations?"

68

"I guess it was done with deliberate intent. Hart knows exactly what he's doing. He figures that if he passes information to me I'll pass some back to him as a *quid pro quo.*"

Lowell gave a little grunt and then puffed at his pipe silently. Neil waited.

"I've been in touch with Washington," Lowell said eventually. "They're going to check Werner's facts and call me back. They're also going to check the defense situation with the Octagon. I told them not to trouble about that.—You scared, Neil?"

"I suppose I am, sir. I haven't had a chance to think about it."

"I'm scared. Unidentified objects. Ten of them. Did Hart tell you there were ten of them?"

Neil nodded.

"Berkeley refused to believe it when Werner made the announcement," Lowell said. "Insisted that they were reflections, or refractions. Space dust." He sighed, and was silent again, as if there were a number of ideas in his mind all scrambling for priority of expression. "Now the whole picture is changed. We spent two and a half hours tonight figuring out our tactics for the meeting tomorrow morning, and we might just as well have saved our breath. Everything's happening too fast. It's a little confusing to an old man like myself.—You're not married by any chance, are you?"

"No, sir."

"That's good. I have an idea this is a time to be unmarried. I have an idea——" He stopped and went on in a calmer voice, "I would like your brother to be here permanently at the Delegation. I've given orders for three rooms to be made ready for him and any equipment he requires to be brought over. I shall be staying on here, and I'd like to be able to consult him whenever I feel it's necessary."

"Mr. Secretary——"

"Are you going to tell me he's sick?"

"He's a very sick man, sir——"

69

"That's what I meant when I asked you if you were married. This isn't a time for emotional attachments."

"Sir, Dr. Ismay will tell you——"

"I know. Dr. Ismay called me yesterday. He told me that Mark has only a few more weeks to live. He asked me to arrange for Mark's appointment as head of the American group to be terminated. I said no."

Neil looked at the older man with bitterness.

Lowell went on, "That's the reason why I made no objection earlier tonight when it was suggested that Mark should be called before the Council of Ministers. I figured Mark would enjoy the experience. Do you think he'd prefer to die in four weeks' time in idleness, or in three weeks' time when he's still working for what he believes in?"

Neil said reluctantly, "I can see that. But it seems a shame——"

"Everything's a shame, Neil. It's a shame that Inter-Cos has turned putrid, and it's a shame that we're in this room wondering what the devil it means that ten unidentified objects are flying toward us. It's all pitiful, my boy." The teleset bell rang, and he leaned over to answer it. He listened and said calmly, "Thank you," and switched off.

He relit his pipe, his cheeks hollowing as he sucked in the smoke. Then he said, "Washington confirms Werner's statement. And the Octagon has confirmed the defense situation. They can't send up any interceptors without permission from Combined Defense here at InterCos."

"But the sooner we find out what's happening the better!" Neil cried.

"InterCos is responsible for global defense," Lowell said calmly. "And you mustn't forget, the President of InterCos is also our Supreme Commander." He looked toward the closed door and his voice became irritable. "I wish Dwight would come back. We ought to get down to business."

Crandall returned in twenty minutes, flushed and

angry. He slammed the office door and stormed over to Lowell. "Werner!" he said furiously. "My God, that man ought to be shot. He's a menace!"

"What happened?"

"He pulled rank on us."

"How?"

"This confounded Supreme Commander bunk. He read us the relevant Articles from the Covenant of Inter-Cos, all the stuff that gives him complete and absolute control in the event of an emergency. He said that he would inform us of all developments, consult us at all times, but we must realize that any separate national action was absolutely forbidden by the Covenant and final action rested with the Supreme Commander and the Committee of Five——"

"Wait a minute," Lowell said. "Did he actually say that this was such an emergency? That these unidentified objects were definitely hostile?"

"Vernon asked him that point-blank. He answered that so far there was no evidence of any kind except that these things had entered our space zones. There was no evidence of hostility, there was no evidence that they were even related to the Ampiti in any way; but the simple fact that they were trespassers was sufficient reason for him to assume immediately the duties of Supreme Commander. He said there was no reason for panic, and he was fully prepared to answer all questions at the meeting scheduled for tomorrow morning."

Lowell said wearily, "I guess we'd better start all over again.—Neil, I'd like you to ask Berkeley, Vernon, Mc-Allister, and the rest of them if they would care to meet with us for discussions as soon as possible. And I suggest you have coffee and sandwiches sent up, and some anti-sleeping pills. We might go on talking for some time."

"Yes, Mr. Secretary," Neil said.

He went to the teleset, and just as he reached it the bell rang. He switched the screen on. Mark was looking out at him, his huge fleshy face distorted with fury.

"Dwight Crandall there?" the shrill voice demanded.

71

"SecState Lowell there? What's going on? What's this I hear about things flying over Alpha——"

Lowell pushed his way to the screen. He said sternly, "I can't talk to you now. Get some sleep. You'll be busy enough tomorrow," and switched the set off. He smiled at Neil, a gray, tired old man, and said, "Go ahead. It's all yours."

5

MARK arrived before eight o'clock. An InterCos attendant wheeled him carefully into Crandall's office, but his voice could be heard even before the door opened, snarling and whining, "Hurry, damn you, hurry, hurry, *push* this thing, will you?" When he saw the men assembled in the office he stopped the wheel chair abruptly, gaped at them, and said with a burst of malevolent laughter, "Well, well. What do you know—a reception committee. Good morning, gentlemen. Greetings."

They were all still there, except Berkeley who had left the meeting at three-thirty. Lowell, Crandall, Vernon, McAllister, Waterson, Locke, Neil, and the other aides were bleary-eyed, unshaven, doped with antisleep pills, desperately in need of rest, but incapable of relaxing now. They mumbled their good mornings to him.

He said, "Jordan Woolley is down below with a truckful of equipment. Where does it go?"

Crandall stood up slowly and said, "We've given you three rooms. 6507, 6508, and 6509.—Isn't Dr. Ismay with you?"

"Ismay's coming later." Mark heaved round and spoke angrily to the atttendant. "You heard those room numbers. What are you waiting for? Help bring that stuff up, fast. And get half-a-dozen engineers from Communications to give Dr. Woolley a hand hooking it up. *Fast.* Understand?"

SecState Lowell said, "Glad to have you here, Mark."

Mark cackled with laughter. "Been up all night, eh? Playing poker, or something? Never saw a more bedraggled crew in all my life. Look at me. Fresh as a daisy. I've been up all night, too."

He sounded mad and violent, Neil thought, as if his brain was on fire. You could see death hovering over him, leaning on his shoulder; and yet he was bursting with a wild vitality, the violence was pounding out of the sickly white body.

Lowell said, "I'd like you to meet——"

"No time. Get to know them as we go along. What have you decided to do? That's the important thing."

"We're only just beginning to see our way——"

"Fine. Fine. Exactly what I expected. *Just beginning* —Neil! Come and push this damned two-wheel hearse for me. It's drafty by this door." He chuckled at Lowell. "I'm sick, you know. Have to take care of my health." And as Neil silently began to push the wheel chair he said, "Over there. Next to my good friend Dwight Crandall. Howdy, Dwight, howdy. Fine weather we're having for this time of the year, eh?"

Crandall said in embarrassment, "Yes, Mark."

Vernon walked to the door saying, "Excuse me. I'd better return to my Delegation." He was angered by Mark's insolence.

"Don't go," Mark shouted. He thumped his hand against the frame of the wheel chair, exploding with rage. "I guess you've spent hours talking a lot of nonsense. Now let's spend a few minutes talking some common sense." He began to cough, glaring at Vernon.

SecState Lowell said, "Perhaps I'd better explain this situation, Mark. We're more or less in Werner's hands. In a crisis like this he's entitled to take over complete control. As President of InterCos he's Chief Executive, Supreme Commander, everything else. The Council of Ministers now has to elect a Committee of Five to serve under him; and it's a pretty sure thing that the five will be Balatov, Hsuen, Dhevu, Vernon, and Crandall, representing the five major power blocs."

Mark spluttered, "I know all this."

74

"Let me finish. The President has the power to over-rule the Committee of Five. However, if the Committee agrees that the emergency is sufficiently serious it can appeal to the Council of Ministers for the election of a new President—which means, in effect, the impeachment of the old one; and the Council is then obliged to take a secret ballot. What we've been trying to do all night is find some way to swing the Committee of Five to our side and force the ballot so that we can get rid of Werner."

Mark said coldly, "And then what?"

"Then put one of our people in. We've agreed on Vernon."

Mark repeated, "And then what, and then what?"

Lowell looked flustered. "Then? Why, then——" He stopped.

Mark sneered, "Then Vernon will order an attack against the Ampiti, eh, instead of Werner ordering it?"

Crandall cried, "For heaven's sake be sensible, Mark. You know we're trying to avoid any sort of conflict."

"So is Werner. You think Werner wants to fight the Ampiti? He's just as scared of conflict as you are. But what are your *plans*, dammit, what are your *plans?* There are the Ampiti, over your heads, and probably a lot more of them on the way, and you people are talking about electing another President. What's this President going to *do*, Lowell?"

Lowell said gravely, "We will assure the Ampiti that we want peace, that we don't want war. We will assure them that we seek universal brotherhood in its profound-est sense——"

"Bosh," Mark said. "Fiddlesticks. Werner will say exactly the same the minute he's convinced the Ampiti mean business. Tweedledum and Tweedledee. There's nothing to choose between either of you." He called in his shrill voice, "Mr. Vernon? Which of you is Mr. Vernon?"

At the door Vernon said, "Yes?"

"There you are. Look, Mr. Vernon, if you become President of InterCos—which makes you the political head of this stupid world—what kind of program do you propose to put over that's different from Werner's program? Eh? So the Ampiti will quietly go home?"

"Dr. Harrison, my program would be as SecState Lowell has stated, assurances of our peaceful intentions, and hopes of peaceful collaboration. As you point out, Dr. Werner would probably offer the same assurances. The difference is, sir, that ours would be honest. I do not think that Dr. Werner's would be honest. That's all."

Mark stared at him narrowly. "Yeah? And how the hell are you going to explain that to the Ampiti?"

"By broadcasts."

"In what language?"

"All languages."

Mark laughed. "This I hope to hear, gentlemen. A broadcast in Esperanto explaining that you've got rid of the nasty old gang and now you have a different gang all good and honest, and please, Ampiti, go away, come back another day." The scorn overflowed in his words. "Now then. Now, then, let's stop being so noble, and let's stop being diplomats, and let's face facts." He said in a louder voice, "Incidentally, Neil, I told Libby not to come back to work any more. I told her to get out of New York fast, and go back to her folks in Podunk, or wherever they live. I hope she takes my advice."

Neil suddenly stiffened.

"All right," Mark snorted. "Facts. Let's take first things first. Who's the Benedict Arnold in this outfit?"

Vernon said in surprise, "What?"

"*You've* heard of Benedict Arnold," Mark sneered. "Who is it that's informing the Ampiti of what's going on here?"

Crandall said, also in surprise, "I'm not sure I understand you, Mark."

"You don't?" Mark shouted. He seemed to quiver all over with the effort of controlling himself. He went on stormily, "Look, Dwight. It didn't happen by coincidence. It *couldn't* happen by coincidence. Try to figure it out for yourself. We began to hear the Voices about a year ago. What was happening at that time? Werner was pushing work on the Beta Platform. If I'm right—and I know I'm right—the Voices were protesting. They didn't want Beta out in space, threatening them. For all we know they may have begun their broadcasts a year or more before we picked them up; maybe as far back as when the original plans for Beta were approved. But how did they find out about Beta?"

Neil watched him, huge and flabby, wriggling in the wheel chair as he spoke.

"It's possible they could see something going on around New Panama," he continued. "The sites being cleared, and so on. Maybe they had their own reconnaissance platforms watching all the activity, and made a shrewd guess what it meant. So they had to find means to warn us not to go ahead with Beta, or any similar project. But hasn't any one of you asked himself, 'Why did the Voices suddenly grow so much louder in the past few weeks; why did they jump forward thirty million miles yesterday when you diplomats were debating the Beta time schedule; why did these ten objects come flying through the sky just when Werner was about to force through the vote on the time schedule; why everything is happening so pat?' Didn't it strike any of you that this was remarkable, to say the least?"

Crandall swore under his breath.

Mark went on, "These sessions of the Council of Ministers are secret, aren't they?" He was beginning to wheeze.

Lowell said, "Yes. They're secret."

"How did the Ampiti discover the critical nature of these secret sessions? How did they come to pick today to show their strength? Coincidence? Or by some kind of extrasensory perception? Or are they being kept informed by somebody inside InterCos?"

"But that's fantastic," Lowell said.

Mark shouted in rage, "Mr. Secretary! Don't tell me it's fantastic unless you can show me where my reasoning is false."

Locke, the New Zealander, spoke for the first time. "Dr. Harrison, we ought to take this one step at a time. Rule out coincidence. The next thing you suggest is extrasensory perception. What about that?"

"I don't know," Mark said angrily. "I don't know because to start with I don't understand the nature of the Ampiti and neither does anybody else in this room. Maybe they're possessed of capabilities of that kind. Maybe they can roam around in space and pick up information wherever they choose. I doubt it. My opinion is that they would more likely use a medium—one mind, one person, with whom they're in constant communication. —What's your name, sir?"

"Locke. New Zealand."

Mark smiled cunningly. "Mr. Locke, you may know more about the subject than I do. I've tried experiments on those lines myself in an attempt to reach the Ampiti, but I haven't been successful." He looked around the room with a leer. "I've never underrated the Ampiti. I've never called them space idiots. So I'm prepared to admit the possibility that they have highly developed extrasensory powers, and can pick the brain of somebody sitting here in the seats of the mighty without that person being conscious of it. I only hope not. I sincerely hope not."

McAllister said loudly, "Why not?"

Mark sneered, "Your name, sir?"

"McAllister. Canada."

"I'll tell you, Mr. McAllister. Because I should like to see the poor, stupid, misled human race get out of this mess you people have landed it in."

"For Pete's sake," Crandall cried, "talk to the point, Mark, talk to the point. What are you driving at?"

Mark sat struggling with his fury. He said at last, "The point is this. I hope there's somebody in InterCos who hates every one of you as much as I do, for your petty conniving, your petty maneuvering, your petty politics, your selfish concern with your own miserable interests—even though of all the groups in this rotten outfit you possibly have the least on your conscience. And

I hope it's this particular somebody in InterCos who's keeping the Ampiti informed, step by step, of all your plots and all your schemes. That's your only chance. Because if you can find this somebody, and you can convince him you really mean what you say, you really want peace, you really want universal brotherhood in its profoundest sense, that you aren't just trying to get a jump ahead of the Russians or the Chinese or the Indians, why——." He began to pant weakly. "—Why, maybe he'll communicate your assurances to the Ampiti and you won't be blown to Kingdom Come, and some of you will live long enough to appreciate what life means."

Lowell said, after the echoes of this violence had died away, "Mark, you have to believe me. We're honest about this."

"Mr. Secretary, I'm willing to grant that you're honest enough not to cut your own grandmother's throat. That's all."

"Thanks, my friend," Lowell smiled.

Mark snarled at Neil, "Get me out of here. I want to see what the dickens Jordan Woolley is doing."

But just as the wheel chair reached the door he swung round again and called, "Lowell!"

"Yes?"

"Take my advice. Don't let anybody in Washington push any buttons. Don't send up any interceptors. Keep clear of the Ampiti. Understand?"

"We can't make any military moves without orders from the Supreme Commander at InterCos," Lowell said. "I've already told you that."

"Good," Mark said. "What are you waiting for, Neil? Get going. I have work to do. Rub the sleep out of your eyes. Move."

He began to hum tunelessly as the wheel chair rolled out into the corridor.

The previous day the Council had met in a mood of surly uneasiness, faced by the deep-rooted conflicts between the Great Powers and the quarrels, the bickering between the smaller nations. But, in a sense, there had still been an overwhelming confidence in their collective destiny. The cosmos seeped through the mural-covered glass walls. The universe outside was waiting for Man to seize it in triumph. Only the decisions had to be taken.

Today the mood was different. The Ministers sitting in the magnificent domed chamber (honorable Ministers Plenipotentiary, armed with full powers to make the gravest decisions on behalf of their respective governments) waited in strained silence for the President to open the Extraordinary General Session. Most of them, Neil could see, had not slept during the night. They had gathered together in groups, like the men in Crandall's office, to try to formulate some course of action which would make them the masters of these strange events. They were grim and silent now. They seemed, individually, filled with resentment, each man hostile toward every other man. And they were waiting, with their advisors beside them, to be reassured that the Ampiti and the Voices and the unidentified objects were merely somebody's wild imaginings, that reality was what it had always been and what it would always continue to be.

There was no applause when Dr. Werner took his place at the podium. He looked surprisingly fresh. Reports had been coming into his office all night; he had held conference after conference wth Ministers, with engineers, with committees and subcommittees; he had been in constant communication with Platform Alpha and New Panama; and yet he looked more alert than ever, his step was jaunty, his eyes were clear, and Neil could have sworn that he was smiling when he began to speak.

He wasted little time after the customary opening, the formula of greeting to the Ministers and other honorable personages present. He went directly to the point.

"In the past twelve hours there have been several remarkable developments which I now propose to review so that the exact sequence may be clear to you, and

80

also so that there may be no mistake as to what these developments imply.

"First, as the Ministers are aware, the Secret Executive Session held last night was interrupted by the information that the so-called Voices of the Ampiti (Ompiti?) had moved forward some twenty-five to thirty million miles. I had intended to play you a recording made at that time; but there have been a number of interesting changes and I have a later recording, taped only an hour ago, which I think will fully illustrate the present position in regard to this particular manifestation; and I will play this tape in a moment or two."

Get going, Neil thought angrily. *Get on with it. Cut out the fancy lace trimmings.*

"Second," Dr. Werner continued, "as I informed all Ministers on receipt of these reports, five unidentified objects were discovered last night by New Panama, flying approximately twenty thousand miles west of the observatory in the direction of Earth; and another five had in some manner reached Platform Alpha, and were located circling approximately a thousand miles overhead, where they still are. I have now to inform you that New Panama has lost contact with the group it originally reported, and these five objects have not so far been relocated. However, a new group has since been reported by New Panama, also flying toward Earth. For technical reasons an exact count has been difficult; but after several checks, the observatory reports the number of machines as 131, and their apparent speed as roughly two thousand miles an hour."

Neil gasped. It was part of a great gasp that puffed through the Council Chamber like a sudden gust of wind. *One hundred and thirty one machines.* . . .

"Third," Dr. Werner went on calmly, "I suggested last night that it might be advisable to maintain a radar watch for any strange objects closely approaching Earth. This radar watch has started already in several countries, and up to this time I have received reports from Hythe, England; Tours, France; and Tokyo, Japan that such objects were picked up by their radar between the hours of four and six this morning."

Crandall sprang to his feet. "Why were we not informed of these facts immediately, Mr. President?"

"You are being informed at the earliest possible opportunity, Mr. Crandall."

"I ask for an immediate recess so that I can inform and consult with my government, Mr. President."

Werner said smoothly, "I hope the honorable Minister can remain patient for a little while longer. I believe that upon reflection he will agree that this is in every respect a global matter and, even more an interspatial matter, on which InterCos is by agreement the supreme authority. Will the honorable Minister kindly recall the Covenant of InterCos, which his government freely signed, in which this is the first Article? And will he kindly recall that Article Five clearly states that the first responsibility of each Minister serving at InterCos shall be not to his national interests but to the interests of all the peoples of the world?"

Crandall sat back fuming at the rebuke.

"I apologize for the interruption," Dr. Werner said. He seemed to dismiss Crandall from his thoughts, as if he were in no way disturbed by Crandall's obvious attempt to disrupt the session.

He said reflectively, "We should now go on to consider the implications of this sudden activity around us; and I think we should at this point listen to the recording which I mentioned a moment ago." He looked around the Chamber with an oddly cheerful expression. "If I may be permitted, I should like to make one observation first. Last night we were somewhat surprised to learn that these Voices had moved forward a very considerable distance—as I said, twenty-five to thirty million miles. During the night this process continued, in a manner not as yet explained. The recording you are about to hear apparently emanated—as closely as our experts can calculate—no more than forty thousand miles from Earth."

He stepped back and pressed a switch.

In the split second before the sound poured out Neil had a frantic impulse to close his ears somehow, to close his ears and shut out the too-near menace, to close his ears and his eyes and all his senses and somehow escape from this assemblage of dignified and eloquent madmen. It was a split second of pure horror in which he found himself at the vortex of a nightmare—the stairs in front of him were covered with little flames, the precipice below his feet was trembling like a jelly, the rocket was altering its course in mid-air to home on his body; and all around him the white faces of the wise madmen ignored his predicament and remained engrossed in contemplation of their navels, heedless of the tottering universe.

But when the sound began this instant of fear immediately passed, and he found himself amazed and intrigued and even amused, like a child in a dentist's chair diverted by the dentist's legerdemain before the drill is applied to the hollow tooth. The Voices were not a roar of anger. They sounded like a chorus, musical and unmusical, each member of the chorus singing or mumbling or calling out an entirely different theme. There seemed to be thousands of these individual themes, and Neil could have sworn that he heard snatches of German, of French and Greek and Italian, Spanish, English, Chinese; words and phrases which he could not specifically identify but which had the timbre of familiarity:

I say old boy, I say old boy, I say old boy . . .

Frère Jacques, Frère Jacques, don-mez vous, dor-mez vous . . .

aleph, beth, gimel, daluth . . . aleph, beth, gimel, daluth . . .

gesundheit, owchoo . . . gesundheit, owchoo, owchoo, owchoo . . .

the square on the side of the hippopotamus . . .

lam min nun ha waw . . . lam mim nun ha waw . . .

hominem quaero . . . fidus Achates . . .

I say old boy, I say ole boy, I thay oly boyly . . .

a riverderci toot-toot . . . a riverderci toot-toot . . .

83

pip-pip, pip-pip . . . pipadapi padapipadapipa . . . pip-
pip . . .
 ici ici ici . . . I say old boy . . . ici ici ici . . . ole boyly . . .
 aleph beth gimel daluth lam mim nun ha waw . . .

There was the faraway wispy echo of a trumpet, the
plucking of strings, a sustained sound like a choking
cockerel, catcalls, a voice that seemed to sing the opening
bars of an operatic aria—*figaro hee, figaro they, figaro
hee, figaro they*—a descending bass voice humming *Ho
Ho Ho Ho* and a quavery soprano squeaking *Ha-ha
Ha-ha Ha-ha Ha-ha.* But it was all a medley, bewilder-
ingly without sense; and when Dr. Werner switched it
off and stood facing his audience with raised eyebrows,
the Ministers began to laugh.

He waited for a few moments and then raised a hand
gracefully imploring silence.

He waited for a few moments and then raised a hand
this fragment from the latest tape made by our engineers
of the Ompiti—Ampiti—Voices. There is a great deal
more; but I can assure you that it is all the same. It
would not be unfair, I think, to describe these sounds
as the sounds of Bedlam."

His arms were outstretched, gripping the waist-high
rail of the podium. "Let us, however, consider this situation very carefully now. Laughter is not enough. The
approach of these maniacal voices through space has a
more serious aspect, for it implies the movement of
apparatus to produce the transmitted radio signals. We
must bear in mind, therefore, that in this alone we have
evidence of a quite fantastic feat of logistics—I use the
word advisedly—the transportation of such apparatus over
a distance of hundreds of millions of miles in a remark-
ably brief period of time; a feat, I must point out, which
we ourselves could not possibly duplicate."

The Ministers were silent again, somber.

"We have also," Werner continued, "the authenticated
reports of first, small numbers, and now a comparatively
large number of objects which have entered our space
zones. We would be foolish to look up at the skies in

84

openmouthed wonder. We are forced to regard these visitors with suspicion. There is no evidence of friendly intent. There is, on the contrary, some evidence of an ugly, brawling, aggressive intent. These objects are trespassers, and for the purposes of self-preservation we must assume that what we are witnessing is a maneuver of encirclement and until we have evidence to disprove it we must also assume that this maneuver is being carried out by a hostile power: the so-called Ampiti."

There was no movement and no other sound in the Chamber, only the echoes of Werner's voice.

"In these circumstances we have unfortunately only one course of action, and that is to declare a state of emergency. This I now do, with a firm sense that history will support my decision; but this I now do with pain, with the utmost sorrow, and with a sense of shame that as President of InterCos, as custodian of Earth's most noble dreams, this step has been forced on me by the hostile act of a horde of barbarians."

He paused. The Ministers seemed frozen with disbelief.

"I must now outline the measures that must follow automatically and immediately. The Council of Ministers will proceed to elect a Committee of Five, which will act as the Cabinet of Defense. The President of Inter-Cos, under Article Eleven of the Covenant of InterCos, becomes Supreme Commander of all national, global, and extraterrestrial forces; but it is my duty to inform you that at the request of the Committee of Five you may by secret ballot replace the Supreme Commander if you are dissatisfied with his conduct of affairs. Until that occurs he is enforced to hold that position and he is enforced to carry out all its obligations. I have already, therefore, in the interests of security, alerted certain defenses and taken other steps which I will be happy to communicate to your representatives as soon as they are elected. That is not all."

He paused again, looking over the heads of the Ministers as if he were looking far beyond, beyond the ob-

85

scured walls, beyond the limits of the city and the land and the ocean.

"I beg of you, to think for one moment as you sit here about the spiritual aspects of the present situation. We have been forced to declare a state of emergency and to take certain precautionary measures because of a fear that we are being menaced. Why are we being menaced at this particular time? The suggestion has repeatedly been made here that the noises made by the Ampiti are an expression of antagonism directed against Earth, that they have been a warning to us not to extend our explorations beyond Mars. The suggestion is being made now that these interloping forces have entered our space zones for the specific reason that we were on the point of launching Platform Beta. We have no way of knowing whether these ingenious theories are correct."

He smiled bitterly. "Let us assume that they are correct. We would then be justified in asking ourselves, What have we done wrong? What fault have we committed? Yesterday, in my address to this Chamber, I gave a brief history of mankind's accomplishments in the past five decades. I told of the fulfillment of many magnificent dreams—the birth of Platform Alpha, the first steps of mankind outward to the Moon, then to Mars. I hinted at our hopes for Mars—that barren planet which we shall transform into a garden, applying all our technology to fostering life where no life was before. Is this how we have sinned? Is this some evil, which has brought armies from outer space to halt us before we can commit greater evils? Have we so disgraced ourselves that we must not be permitted to pollute other planets beyond Mars, other systems beyond our own system? Are our intentions so vile that we must be fenced in like wild animals, like wild animals that must not be allowed to roam at large through the Universe?"

He looked at Dhevu, at Hsuen and Balatov and Vernon and Crandall; and his mouth tightened. Neil could feel a tiny stirring, a movement in the frozen hall as if men were awakening from sleep.

"I stand here," Werner said, "addressing a noble assemblage. This assemblage has only one purpose: to act in the interests of humanity as a whole. Yet each one of you remains bound in his heart to some special area on the earth's surface where a special warmth, a special love exists for him. And each of you takes pride in the special achievements of his nation. Shall I enumerate some of them? Would it be possible to enumerate the achievements of the Indian nation, with a culture that was superb even before recorded history, of the Chinese whose culture is equally ancient and equally splendid, of the Russians whose musicians and writers have been without parallel, of the French whose very name has been synonymous with culture, of the Italians, the great Turks, the amazing Arab peoples, the Japanese and the Mexicans and the British?"

His voice rose, lashing out in a storm of rage. "That is what we carry with us when we go out on our explorations in the darkness of space, a heritage of culture, a heritage of almost divine achievement, of poems and music, of sacred dance and sacred philosophy, of science and technical power, of strength and understanding. This is the heritage that came to fulfillment with the building of the Palace of InterCos, this is the banner we raise wherever we go. And who opposes us now? Who demands that we stay behind our fence like wild animals? The Ampiti. Listen to them! The self-appointed guardians of space."

He switched the recording on again, the sounds of Bedlam.

I say old boy . . . I say old boy . . .
Ho ho ho ho . . . ha-ha ha-ha ha-ha ha-ha . . .
pipadapipadapipadapipa . . .
mooooo-moooooooooooo . . .
kobley-kobley, kobley-kobley, pipadapipa . . .
aleph, beth, gimel, daluth, aleph beth, gimel, daluth . . .
hee-hee, hu-hu, hee-hee, hu-hu . . .
Abdada-abdada, nu-nu-nu . . .

And, abruptly and scornfully, he switched the noise off.

"Those are the Voices which, if Dr. Harrison's theory

87

is correct, intend to impose on us a limit beyond which we must not go. I do not wish to argue with this theory. I can only say, if this theory is correct then God help us all because it means the end of our dream, it means even more—it means, in my opinion the enslavement of humanity by barbarians.

"The session is now open for debate."

Balatov began the applause, and nearly every man in the Chamber rose at once to give Werner an ovation. Even Neil could not help feeling admiration for him as he stood alone on the podium. It was possible to disagree with him, it was possible to hate him, but it was not possible to despise him. He had concealed nothing. He had clearly stated alarming new facts to an audience which was already alarmed. There was the threat of ruin to all his plans and all his hopes, and yet he had risen to that threat in a remarkable way. His eloquence was the eloquence of courage, and Neil had the impression that every person present had caught some of the fire from him. SecState Lowell, Crandall and Vernon remained seated, but they looked disturbed as if the President's speech had impressed them and had left them with little that they could say in reply. Berkeley was clapping warmly, and Dhevu had risen with Hsuen and Balatov.

Werner received the applause without any sign of emotion. He bowed stiffly, and then holding up his hand for silence said, "The Chair recognizes the honorable Minister Plenipotentiary from the Russian Union." Balatov had been the first to rise; he was still standing and Werner was therefore correct in calling upon him.

When the Chamber was seated and quiet Balatov said, "Mr. President, from all that we have heard it is clear that there is undoubtedly a great deal for us to discuss in this meeting. With all due respect, however, before we begin debate, I beg to offer the following resolution: That this session of the Council of Ministers meeting in the Palace of InterCos wishes to express its fullest confidence in the leadership of the President of the Council.

I request, Mr. President, that a vote on this resolution be taken immediately."

There was a shout of approval. The Lord Hsuen rose to second the resolution.

Crandall stood up. Werner said calmly, "The Chair recognizes the honorable Minister Plenipotentiary from the United States."

The Chamber became silent.

Crandall said, "Mr. President, it is my painful duty to oppose the resolution now on the floor. No doubt the honorable Minister who has proposed this resolution has been moved, as many of us have, by the clear and forceful speech of the President of the Council; but we are not voting approval of a speech, we are voting approval of a policy. Only when we have carefully examined this policy and drawn our conclusions from it can we express confidence or lack of confidence in the leadership of InterCos. I therefore propose that the resolution before us shall be postponed until the Chamber has had an opportunity to debate, carefully and in detail, the speech from the Chair."

Unexpectedly, the Brazilian Minister rose to second Crandall's motion. With the utmost serenity Dr. Werner proceeded with the formalities of taking the vote.

The result was obvious, even before the voting began. Balatov was supported by a large majority. But there were several notable abstentions, Neil noticed. The Indian Minister had evidently reconsidered his position, and had refrained from voting on either side. So had the Turkish and French Ministers. To this extent Crandall had scored a small victory.

Balatov then proposed the immediate election of the Committee of Five. Crandall opposed him with the same arguments, demanding a debate first. The wearying process began again; and again Balatov was successful. Then came the slow-footed mechanical process of balloting—the proposing of candidates, the elimination of candidates, the flowery speeches of introduction; and the morning died. The Five, as expected, were Balatov, Hsuen, Dhevu, Crandall, and Vernon.

89

Neil waited for the next move. It came from the Polish Minister. He said, "As the President so forcibly explained in his speech, we are faced with what is clearly an invasion of our space zones. While debate on the situation is desirable, such debate could continue indefinitely while the situation became more critical. I propose therefore that we elect an acting President, and that the Supreme Commander and the Committee of Five immediately retire to carry out their duties; and that the debate to which we are committed be held with the acting President in the chair."

The Chamber agreed. The morning session ended.

Neil walked back to the Delegation office with Crandall and SecState Lowell. He should have felt indifferent to the successes and the failures he had witnessed. This, after all, was something he had been participating in for a long time: somebody had to win, somebody had to lose, and generally in the end there was a kind of tacit compromise which took the sting out of defeat. Generally, too, the final result appeared not too harmful to all concerned, which meant the entire human race. But now, when no echo remained of Werner's eloquence, he felt as if he were walking into a dense fog. He was losing his sense of direction; and even the two men beside him could give him no assurance of a safe arrival anywhere.

6

THE FIRST announcement of the Committee of Five came at three o'clock and was read to the Council of Ministers by the acting President. It stated simply: "All work relating to the Beta Complex has been suspended indefinitely at the following InterCos installations: Sahara, Lake Baikal, Platform Alpha, New Panama."

SecState Lowell had taken Crandall's place on the Council. He looked pleased when the announcement was read, and whispered to Neil, "That's something, at least. Score one for us."

At three-thirty there was a further bulletin to interrupt the debate. This, too, was simple: "The Committee of Five has requested the well-known authority on twentieth-century radio techniques, Dr. Olaf Johanassen, to take charge of the entire program of InterCos space broadcasts. This appointment comes into immediate effect."

SecState Lowell turned inquiringly to Neil.

Neil said, "That's the professor whom Werner laughed at yesterday. Johanassen put forward the theory that the Ampiti were twentieth-century radio echoes."

"Oh, no!" SecState Lowell whispered. "They can't do that. Mark was the only man for that job, or one of his associates."

"Score one for them," Neil said. "All even."

The debate was slow. It seemed as if the Ministers recognized that they had been stripped of power and

91

that their words and arguments were without any real meaning. The only deliberations that could affect present issues were those of the six men now in a room that was in a sense antipodal to the Council Chamber. The dome of the Chamber was often enveloped in cloud. The meeting place of the Committee of Five was ninety feet below ground level, deep in Manhattan granite.

At four o'clock the acting President read another bulletin. *"One:* All new flights between Earth, Platform Alpha, and New Panama, in either direction, are hereby canceled. *Two:* All craft now in transit are ordered to display continuously flashing white identification lights, and are ordered to land within the shortest possible time, even if this implies reversing course. *Three:* All interceptor craft, without exception, are hereby grounded."

"Thank God," Lowell murmured.

Twenty minutes later there was an amendment to this bulletin. "All interceptor craft shall remain grounded but are permitted to take on fuel and other requisites. Craft so prepared may be moved out of hangars."

"Balatov is taking no chances," Neil said.

"Trouble," SecState Lowell said gloomily. "Trouble."

Another amendment came within ten minutes. "Interceptor craft are forbidden to load any f-material. Repeat: interceptor craft are forbidden to load any f-material. The ban on the movement of all f-material remains strictly in force."

Debate was impossible. Ministers stood up to speak, began with passion and then lost the power to utter consecutive sentences. The acting President appeared to be waiting only for new bulletins to arrive. The last came at two minutes to five, and the Council gasped when the message was read. "The Committee of Five announces that specific contact has been made with the craft which have entered our space zones. No further information can be given at the present time."

The acting President ordered the session closed.

SecState Lowell was silent until he and Neil reached Crandall's office. Then, very slowly and deliberately he lit his pipe and sat down on the corner of Crandall's desk.

He said, "Well?"

"Sir?"

"What did that last bulletin mean, Neil?"

"That's anybody's guess, Mr. Secretary. And I imagine it was framed precisely in that way in order to make it anybody's guess."

Lowell repeated the words, turning them over on his tongue as if he were tasting some strange wine. *"The Committee of Five announces that specific contact has been made with the craft which entered our space zones.* So. Contact. What sort of contact? Verbal? Or are we within firing range? Are we going to talk or are we going to fight, or what?"

Neil said, "Isn't that why the bulletin was so ambiguous? The Committee of Five isn't sure itself."

"They grounded all interceptor craft."

Neil looked at him curiously. He said, "Interceptor craft aren't the only fighting machines we possess, sir. There are about twenty-five battle wagons under Inter-Cos command. None of the bulletins made any reference to those."

Lowell puffed away silently. After a few moment he said, "I'd forgotten about battle wagons. Weren't they put away in a cave somewhere? None of them has been flown for the past thirty years, I understood."

"Ultimate defense," Neil said. "They can be readied for action in a few hours."

"Big things," Lowell said reflectively. "I remember them now. *Big* things."

"When I was a kid we used to play with models of them," Neil said. "Mark once described them to me. He figured one would be sufficient to defend our entire eastern seaboard, for example. A couple of them would be enough to protect Platform Alpha, or New Panama. They carry about a hundred and fifty interceptors each, apart from other weapons."

Lowell said, "All right. Let's clear the blood from our

93

eyes, that's only one possibility. Suppose the bulletin means we've established specific verbal contact?"

"We've started diplomatic conversations, in that case."

Lowell said sharply, "In what language? You heard that last tape, didn't you? It sounded like a barnyard." He eased himself off the table. "Let's look in on Mark."

Neil opened the door for him, but as Lowell reached it he stopped suddenly, his face drawn with pain, and said, "Even if we *know*, even if it's *true* that Werner has ordered battle wagons up, what can we do? We can't stop him now. We're helpless."

He walked out, stiff-legged; and Neil followed him.

In Room 6507 Jordan Woolley was watching the screen of an oscilloscope. He did not hear them enter.

Neil said, "Hello, Jordan."

Woolley swung round. His eyes were blank, as if he were only half-awakened from a dream. He said, "Hi, Neil," and then, recognizing Lowell, stood up respectfully.

"We're looking for Mark," Neil explained.

"I think you'll find him in 6509. That's where I saw him last. He was working with a computer."

Lowell said, "Thank you," and began to walk away. But the flickering line on the screen had intrigued him, and he paused, pointed at it, and asked, "What's that?"

"A recording of the Voices, sir."

"The latest recording? Those barnyard noises?"

Woolley laughed nervously. "Yes, Mr. Secretary."

"Ah." Lowell leaned forward, staring at the pulsating image as if it might reveal something valuable to him. He said, "Tell me, Dr. Woolley, have you found the slightest evidence of any meaning in that racket?"

"No, sir," Woolley answered. "It's baffling." He sounded even more nervous and his eyes had clouded over again.

"Is that so?" Lowell said, and stalked out. In the corridor he said testily to Neil, "So Dr. Woolley is baffled, eh? *Baffled.*"

Neil did not reply.

94

Lowell snorted. "A fine time to be baffled, by God. Just when we need something clear and definite these fool experts act as if they'd never seen a chicken hatch out of an egg."

He tapped at the door of 6509 and opened it. Mark was sitting in his wheel chair, white with rage; and Libby was standing facing him, pale too, with her hands clasped behind her back.

"Lowell!" Mark cried. "Lowell! Just in time. Mr. Secretary, I want you to exert your authority. Have this woman thrown out of here."

Neil said in surprise, "Libby!"

"Hello, Neil." Her voice was weak.

"Don't you speak to her, Neil," Mark raged. "She doesn't have any business here in InterCos. The guards shouldn't have let her through. Have her thrown out."

Lowell stepped between them, like a teacher intervening in a classroom fracas. "Now, now," he said gently. "Now, now. What's going on?"

Neil said, "Mr. Secretary, may I present Dr. Elizabeth Hewes, of the American Astro-Research group."

"She isn't," Mark yelled. "She isn't any longer. She isn't on my staff."

Lowell said courteously, "I'm delighted to make your acquaintance, Dr. Hewes," and held out his hand.

She said, "This is a great honor, Mr. Secretary," and slipped her gloved hand into his.

Lowell turned to Mark. "Now, my friend, what's the trouble?"

"I don't want her, that's all. Throw her out. Get rid of her. She doesn't have any right here. This project is secret. I ought to have protection——" He began to cough, in heavy painful spasms.

"Mark!" Libby cried anxiously.

He waved her away with a wild movement of his huge arm.

She said to Lowell, "Mr. Secretary, I only came to help. He can't do this work alone. He needs more assistance——"

"He seems very upset, Dr. Hewes."

95

Mark struggled with the words. "Get her out of here."

Lowell suggested politely, "Perhaps you could wait in the next room," and she walked away without any protest.

Mark began to relax. He gave a deep sigh, and snuffled as he tried to regain his breath.

Neil said, "What's the matter now, Mark? You've always had a lot of respect for Libby's work."

Mark glowered at him, and turned to Lowell. "Mr. Secretary, I'm relying on you to have her removed. I don't want her hanging around here."

"Why?" Lowell asked, genuinely puzzled.

"I'll tell you why," Mark said. He thrust his head out of the collar of flesh like a snapping turtle. "I like her, that's why. I told her to go back to Podunk, or wherever her home is. She'll be safe there. All hell is likely to break loose here, any minute. I don't want her caught up in it. I've sent Evelyn and the boys up to New Hampshire, too." His head jerked round to glare at Neil. "Satisfied now?"

Lowell said in a puzzled way, "Are you serious, Mark?"

Mark flew into his apoplectic rage. "Mr. Secretary, when I tell you a thing I *mean* it, I'm *serious——*"

"All right," Lowell said hastily. "Hold your horses."

"Listen to me, both of you. Neil, you're fond of Libby, eh? You want to marry her one day? All right. See that she gets out of town as soon as possible. Lowell, you're concerned with the safety of the State? Start making plans to get the women and children out of the big cities. New York. Chicago. Detroit. All the big cities. Call in every expert on transportation you can find. And do it *now*."

"I'd need some good reasons, Mark."

"I don't have any reasons." In agitation he propelled the wheel chair a few yards, and stopped it with the palms of his hands against the wheel spokes. "I don't have any reasons. I only have a hunch. Did you hear the recording of this morning's Voices, Lowell?"

"Yes."

"It scared me.—Has the Council of Ministers heard it?"

"Werner played it to them this morning."

"Werner thought it was funny, eh?"

"Barbaric."

Mark twisted his head again to stare up at Lowell. The small sunken eyes looking up at the older man were perfectly round, colorless, and dead like the eyes of a fish. "You know what I thought?"

"That's partly why I came in to see you."

"It sounded to me like young braves whooping it up. The beginning of a war dance. Shouting catcalls, abuse, jeering at the palefaces. Think that's funny, Mr. Secretary?"

Lowell remained silent.

The swollen lips puckered. "I wasn't expecting it. I thought there'd be more time for negotiation. I thought I'd knock some sense into your head, Crandall's, Vernon's, and maybe we'd be able to work out some clear policy. Get some clear statement from *them,* too." He blinked his dead eyes. "What's happening with the Committee of Five?"

Lowell told him briefly, up to the last bulletin.

Mark sat back mumbling to himself. "That isn't right," he said eventually. "It doesn't sound like Werner. He wouldn't stop all activity at Sahara and Baikal. What else? Has there been anything else?"

"Just one other thing," Lowell said, and he looked at Neil as he spoke. "We had another bulletin a few minutes ago. It merely said the Committee of Five has established specific contact with the craft which have entered our space zones. That's all."

Mark said, "What sort of specific contact?"

"We have no further information."

Mark tried to rise. It was impossible for his weakened legs to support his bulk, but he tried to stand to meet SecState Lowell face to face. He was so violent that Neil sprang forward to prevent the wheel chair from overturning.

Lowell said, "Don't get mad with me, Mark."

97

"The bulletin might be referring to contact for the purpose of conversations," Neil said quickly. He wanted to calm the sick man. "There's no reason to believe——"

Mark was panting. He put one of his hands to his throat, as if this would enable him to control his breath, and said, "There's something I have to tell you, Mr. Secretary. I haven't been able to get much help from Communications Division here—for good reasons, I guess. I've set up my own M-beam transceiver, and I've been relying for all my stuff on our installation at Easthampton. Taylor called me this afternoon, the chief engineer. He had a peculiar radar blip, something like a supercargo ship, the things that have been carrying the Beta sections from Sahara and Lake Baikal to Platform Alpha. He couldn't hold it long enough for identification.–It could have been something else, you know, it could have been something else——"

He made another effort to stand. Neil said, "Sit down, Mark, *sit down*. Take it easy."

"Take it easy!" Mark roared. "Lowell! Listen to me! If Werner is sending up battle wagons I'm warning you here and now, they'll be annihilated. He's crazy. I know those battle wagons. They're antiques compared to what the Ampiti must have. I'm warning you, Lowell, this is going to mean disaster——"

Lowell said, "Wait a minute, Mark." He turned to Neil. "I'd like to talk this over at some length. I also want a record in permanent form." He addressed his question to Mark. "Is there a tape recorder in this room?"

"Ask Jordan Woolley to plug one in," Mark growled. Neil turned to go.

Lowell said to him, "There's no need for you to hang around. I suggest you look after Dr. Hewes——"

"Have her thrown out of here," Mark shouted.

"All right," Neil said, and walked into the adjoining room.

They sat by one of the windows in the lounge, and Libby glanced out at the pale evening sky, the blurred

98

horizon, the torrent of the East River making scars of white on the steel-gray surface; and she said politely, "What a beautiful view."

"Yes," Neil said. "A beautiful view."

She looked slowly and critically around the big lounge, and said in the same polite voice, "What attractive decorations."

"Yes," Neil said. "Very attractive decorations."

Most of the tables were crowded. She asked, "Are all these people on the staff of InterCos?"

"I guess so. We have lots and lots of people on the staff of InterCos."

She said, "I see that many of the girls are wearing dominoes."

"Yes." He did not turn his head.

"There you are," she said. "So you really shouldn't tease me about wearing mine. I think it's a very becoming fashion. Don't you?"

"No, darling."

"You mustn't call me darling. Somebody might come over and question my credentials."

He said, "Would you explain to me how this ridiculous fashion started?"

"Why," she said, "it's meant to conceal the eyes."

"You could wear dark glasses."

"Oh, but we did, once. A hundred years ago. Lots of women wore dark glasses then to conceal their eyes, but I think these dominoes are a lot prettier."

"Why do you need to conceal your eyes, Libby?"

"Because, Neil dear, the eyes are the mirror of the soul—haven't you heard? And these days no unmarried girl like myself wants to have her soul stared at."

They went on talking idly and flippantly, their emotions withheld; and for Neil it was a relief after all the events and all the conversations of last night and today— the benevolent and malevolent scheming, the double cross and the double double cross and the endless treachery of high diplomacy, the subtle battle for supremacy and the subtle skirmishes and the subtle undermining of human spirits. He was tired of the voices of Werner

99

and Balatov and Hsuen, and even of Crandall's voice and Lowell's; he was tired of the voices of the Voices in all their manifestations, the distant, the loud, and the near, the voices that shouted and the voices that wailed and the voices that said so idiotically "I say old boy, I say old boy, I say old boy." He was revolted by the recollection of the domed Council Chamber and the spears of the Universe that constantly penetrated it; and he was revolted by the recollection of Man's triumph, the space ships going out with a roar of rockets, the mad rush through black skies, the fall, the landing, the oiled doors opening upon barren landscapes, the flag of Inter-Cos planted and the subsequent planting of the flags of all the nations of the earth in alphabetical order, the solemn intonation of the formula of annexation, the thin cheers, and the eyes of the conquistadores turned up in bright speculation at the next planet, the next spheroid, the next solar system, beyond and beyond and beyond. He wanted only to sit with this woman, this biological oddity with the dark-blue domino shielding her light-blue eyes, and let the blood run smoothly and warmly through his veins as if life had no other purpose.

He said, "I have my own theory about these dominoes. I think they're a challenge."

She said, "Really?"

"Yes. They say to a man, *Hey, you! See if you're smart enough to get past me.*"

"Oh no," Libby said. "I don't think so." She sounded as if she were a trifle shocked by his suggestion. She sounded very ladylike; but he could see her eyes twinkling, as if she were pleased and amused by this flirtation.

He said, "I have such a yearning to take the thing off."

"Neil!" she said.

"How does it fasten? With a knot, or a bow, or a clasp?"

"I couldn't possibly tell you such intimate details."

He said, "Libby."

"Yes?"

"If I could escape from this place for a couple of hours tomorrow, would you marry me?"

She was laughing at him. "Oh, my poor boy."

"Would you?"

"Oh, Neil," she said. "Oh, Neil. If it matters to you so much I'll tell you. It fastens with a clasp."

He was laughing too. "I thought it was a bow.—Will you marry me?"

"Tomorrow?"

"At dawn," he said. "At sunrise, if possible."

They were laughing at each other like children.

"What a wonderful idea," she said; and then she said, "No."

"The day after tomorrow?"

She sighed. "No."

"One week from tomorrow?"

"No."

"Libby!"

"But how could I, Neil? How could I?" All the lightness had gone from her voice. She sounded now as if she were in pain.

"I think we'd be good together."

"Yes. I know we'd be good together—if. If it were a normal world, if we could forget so many of the things we've learned. I'm so frightened, Neil."

He saw that the shadows had returned.

She leaned forward anxiously, trying to make something clear to him. "I'm not frightened for myself, Neil. I'm frightened for you, and for Mark and for Evelyn, and for all the millions of people who don't know what's happening, what's going to happen to their harmless little lives. Something's gone so terribly wrong."

"You're worrying about it too much——"

"Am I?"

"Yes."

She said, with just the ghost of a smile, "I ought to explain. I'm not a very good woman for you, my dear, my nerves are stretched too tight, my brain works too hard. But—oh, Neil, I'd be overjoyed to marry you and forget all my stupid problems, and spend the rest of my life worrying only about your happiness, and bear you children and—don't you see?"

"Don't I see what?"

She said helplessly, "You're so confident. You're not afraid——." She clasped her hands against her body. "Very well. I'll try to be confident, too. If it isn't too late in a week's time I'll marry you then."

He smiled at her. "And you'll never wear a domino again?"

Her laughter came with difficulty. "Never."

He said, "I feel such affection for you—I can't tell you about it here. Do you believe me?"

"I believe you. I feel terribly deep affection——." Her voice seemed to fade.

"Now we understand each other," he said. "And now I want you to do something for me.—Where does your family live?"

"In Richmond, Virginia."

He said gaily, "Not Podunk?"

"Not Podunk."

"That's good. I want you to go and stay with them in Richmond, Virginia, until I can come and join you there."

She said, "And I thought you were so confident!"

"I am, I am. But——"

"No," she said. "I shan't leave New York."

"Please, Libby."

"I wouldn't go earlier because I felt my place was with Mark. I couldn't possibly go now."

"Just to give yourself a rest," he pleaded.

She said, "How can you ask a woman who loves you—who feels affection for you—to do something like that?"

"For my peace of mind."

"What about *her* peace of mind? Mark ordered Evelyn to take the boys up to New Hampshire. She sent the boys. But she's still in the house in Central Park. Would you expect her to leave Mark at a time like this?"

He did not know what to answer.

She said, "I was in the next room, you know. I couldn't

help overhearing Mark when he started to shout about battle wagons."

Neil said in a low, alarmed voice, "Libby, you mustn't talk about that down here——"

"I suppose I shouldn't. I guess InterCos is going to keep this war secret, absolutely secret——"

"Libby!"

"I'm sorry." She sounded wretched. "Couldn't you persuade Mark to let me come and work for him again? Just so that I could be here, near both of you?"

"He won't allow it."

"He needs me," she said desperately. "After all, he's still human. He needs somebody to be kind to him, somebody who understands what he's going through——"

Hart von Horstmann walked gracefully to the table, smiling at both of them. He said with his customary charm, "Neil, pardon me if I intrude——"

Neil said, "Hello, Hart," and stood up angrily. There was no way of evading the young man in these circumstances. He said "Libby, may I present Hart von Horstmann; Hart, Dr. Elizabeth Hewes."

Hart beamed at her. "Dr. Hewes! Dr. Harrison's coworker!"

Neil said, "Yes," forestalling anything she might say.

"I am really enchanted to meet you," Hart said. "As Neil will tell you, I admire Dr. Harrison's work so much. A wonderful man, a wonderful brain. One of these days I hope to have the great pleasure of meeting him personally."

"You're very kind," Libby said.

"I understand that Dr. Harrison has now joined the American Delegation here at InterCos. I am so glad to hear it. Perhaps you can tell me, is he continuing with his experiments to communicate with these strange creatures, the Ampiti?"

She asked, "Which experiments?"

"Wasn't he trying to investigate extrasensory methods?"

"Oh," she said, frowning, "was he? Where did you hear that?"

"Where did I hear it?" He laughed, and then looked

puzzled. "I'm not sure. Perhaps I read it in one of his reports."

"Sit down," Neil said. "Join us, Hart." It would be interesting, he thought, to discover the source of Hart's information.

"Not now, old man," Hart said. "I'm just on my way upstairs."

"What's your hurry?"

"Work, work, work," Hart smiled. "By the way, did you see the news on the agency wires a few minutes ago?"

"What news?"

"A large mass of debris was found off Halifax, Nova Scotia, at noon. Big stuff. Like one of the supercargo space ships. Did you hear?"

Neil stared at him. "No."

"A pretty bad crash, it seems. We haven't had anything like that in twenty-five years." He gave Libby his most dazzling smile. "I'd better run along. It has been a delight to have this pleasure. I most sincerely hope we shall meet again soon, my dear Doctor." He clapped Neil heartily on the shoulder and strode off.

"What on earth does that mean?" Neil said. "Those supercargo ships are as safe as a house. They *can't* crash. It's almost impossible for them to crash——"

Libby asked, "Did you tell him about Mark's extra-sensory experiments?"

"Of course not."

"Who told him, then?"

"I couldn't even guess. He's a tricky character. He picks information out of thin air."

"How could he have heard of Mark's experiments? *Somebody* must have told him?"

"Jordan Woolley?"

"No," Libby said. "Jordan's the most loyal person in the world."

Neil said, "I don't like it. I don't like the way he talks about that, and I don't like the way he threw out the news about this crash. There's something queer——"

His recall plate buzzed.

Libby looked at him, and he looked back at her feeling a deeper intimacy and a deeper affection than he had known before. He said, "That must be SecState Lowell. I have to go."

"Yes, Neil."

"Will you, to please me, take the first plane out to Podunk tonight?"

She smiled. "Richmond, Virginia."

"Very well. Richmond, Virginia. And warn your family that I will be arriving in a few days to claim you?"

"No," she said. "Dear Neil, when you're ready to claim me I'll be waiting in my apartment on Sixtieth Street. Come there."

He said after a moment's pause, "I'll come soon. As soon as I can. Tomorrow, I hope."

She laughed at him. "Tomorrow!"

"If it's possible."

She said gently, with a slight intake of breath, "Very well, my dear," and stood up to leave.

The recall signal was from SecState Lowell. Neil found him in Crandall's room.

He said, "Ismay and Luden arrived a few minutes ago. They're giving Mark his injections, so I had to leave." He smiled palely. "Mark was furious. We'd just received some very interesting news."

"About the crash off Halifax, sir?"

"You already know?"

"Hart von Horstmann told me in the lounge."

"Is that so?" Lowell was thoughtful for a moment. "That young man is being very obliging these days."

Neil said, "Too obliging. I think he's overplaying his hand."

Lowell grunted. He eased himself off the corner of Crandall's desk, walked to the window and looked out, walked back restlessly and sat down in an armchair, his long legs and arms jutting out at all angles. He said, "Mark doesn't seem to believe that it was a supercargo ship that crashed."

"I had the impression Hart was trying to hint at that, too."

"What's your guess?"

Neil said carefully, "I wouldn't even care to guess. It could have been a supercargo ship. Or, possibly, a battle wagon."

"I wish Crandall were here," Lowell cried. "I'd like to know the truth about this. Was it a battle wagon or wasn't it?" He stood up again, irritable and uncertain. "Do you realize that we can't do a thing here? We might as well pack up and go home. We're being run——." He altered the emphasis. "—The *world* is being run by Werner and the Committee of Five in a locked room underground. And InterCos is supposed to be a democratic institution. It isn't. It's a——" He stopped, and then said uncomfortably, "This whole business is getting on my nerves. Not enough sleep, I suppose." He smiled, and then frowned. "I had a long talk with Mark. The tape's on the desk there. Play it back on Crandall's machine."

Neil clipped the tape in position and watched it roll through the automatic loop. The faces of Mark and Lowell appeared on the small screen as each began to speak, but Lowell said, "Cut out the visual, keep it sound only, I don't want to look at my face." Neil touched the visual switch and the screen dimmed. It was like listening to dialogue in a darkened theater: Mark's voice high-pitched and angry, Lowell's calm and reasonable.

LOWELL: I want this for the record, Mark——

MARK: Werner. These battle wagons. It's monstrous——

LOWELL: I repeat, I want this for the record. That's why I'm putting it on tape. Try to control you temper——

MARK: Mr. Secretary——

LOWELL: Now listen, Mark. A lot has been happening in the past forty-eight hours, and it's too much for my simple brain. I'm in a fog. But I have a hunch that all this activity has heightened your reactions and I want the benefit of that, I want to know your thinking. Now calm down, and start from the beginning. Berkeley asked last night, *Who* are the Ampiti? Well?

106

How would you answer that one?

MARK: You want an answer to that one?

LOWELL: Stop being sarcastic.—Yes.

Pause.

MARK: All right. I'll try to answer it. But obviously I don't know. Understand? I don't, you don't, nobody does, except maybe this Benedict Arnold character I assume is in contact with them. Even he probably doesn't know anything about them, they're just using him. But that's the most important point, Lowell. *We don't know.*

LOWELL: Be careful. You say that's the most important point. Why?

MARK: Confound it, I am being careful. It's the most important because all our thinking must be based on that fact. We don't know, therefore it's impossible to predict what they'll do, you can't attach any known kind of personality to them, we can't guess at any behavior pattern.

LOWELL: They must be in some way similar to ourselves, Mark. They've built machines, they fly these machines——

MARK: But the key word is still *unpredictable.*

LOWELL: Explain that.

MARK: It's simple enough. Look. They've been broadcasting nonsense for a year. Then they come bouncing through space saying a few words that sound intelligible, bounce forward a lot nearer with a lot more words that sound intelligible too but are what you might hear in an insane asylum. What comes next? I wouldn't even try to predict.

LOWELL: Yes, I see that——

MARK: Let's go on, then. We don't know who they are, we don't know where they come from. Neptune? Some other system? Possibly. Wherever it is, they've picked up enough information to enable them to make an attempt at communication, to try to master our speech forms——

LOWELL: Master our speech forms?

MARK: It's only a parrot gabble, so far. My guess is that they don't use speech themselves, they communicate among themselves in some other way. Libby thinks they may have built speech machines for our benefit, and I'm inclined to agree with her——

LOWELL: Speech machines?

MARK: Mr. Secretary, if you're going to interrupt every few seconds with these fool remarks——

LOWELL: Go on, go on——

MARK: I'll sum it up like this: Here are these unknown beings. For the past year they've tried to tell us something, as best they could. Their efforts haven't succeeded. We've ignored what they were trying to say, and they've been forced to take other steps to get their ideas over.—Only, remember, Lowell, that's putting Ampiti thinking into terms of human thinking——

LOWELL: Now, don't confuse me——

MARK: You're going to be a sight more confused before they're through with you, my friend.—I'll carry my assumptions a stage further. I maintain that the cause of all this activity is the Beta Complex, and what they've learned about the human race in the past twenty, thirty, forty centuries, or more. I maintain that they want no part of us——

LOWELL: We're not so bad, Mark——

MARK: No?

LOWELL: After all——

MARK: I could weep, Mr. Secretary. I see the history of the human race as a history of chicanery, of deceit and treachery, of rape and murder and the cold-blooded destruction of everything that was noble in the human spirit——

LOWELL: Oh come now——

MARK: Let me have my say, will you?—I see that the mass of human beings at all times has preferred ignorance and slothfulness, and they might just as well not have lived——

LOWELL: We differ about this, you know——

MARK: I see that whenever men of wisdom and courage

108

have arisen it has been necessary to poison them with hemlock or nail them to a cross——

LOWELL: We are talking about the Ampiti——

MARK: We are still talking about the Ampiti.—And I see that the greatest heroes of the human race have always been the greatest killers, Alexander the Great (*Great!*) and Napoleon and——

LOWELL: No. You're wrong. The compulsion of mankind is toward——

MARK: Treachery.

LOWELL: —goodness, achievement, the categorical imperative——

MARK: Mr. Sec—Mr. Secretary—reach me—reach me that water, will you—water.—Ah. Ah. Thank you——

LOWELL: Are you all right, Mark—Mark!

MARK: I'm—I'm——

LOWELL: Sit back, man——

MARK: I'm all right.

LOWELL: Take it easy. I'll switch this thing off.

MARK: Don't do that. Let me finish. I want to say this for the record. Chicanery, Lowell. Double-dealing. Centuries of it. Like the Spaniards and the Incas, but centuries of it. InterCos, now. Look at InterCos. Werner. Going out to conquer the Universe the way the Spaniards conquered the Incas, eh? The largest-scale hijacking operation the eyes of God ever saw——

LOWELL: Relax, Mark. You're tired.

MARK: Just let me tell you. The Ampiti, whoever they are, won't take it. They've seen us in action, and they've decided that we'd better stay where we are. Maybe they think of Earth the way we think of Hell, and they don't want the boundaries of Hell extending too far. And what they'll do next is anybody's guess because, as we agreed, they're unpredictable, and technically they're centuries ahead of us——

A disturbance in the background.

A voice, saying, Mark.

MARK: Can't you see I'm busy, Jordan? Get out of here.

JORDAN: Griff Luden and Bernie Ismay are here, Mark.

MARK: Tell them to wait. Get out.

JORDAN: Just a minute. There's something else. You ought to know about it. I just took it off the wire services——

MARK: What?

JORDAN: The Canadian Coast Guard reports finding extensive wreckage thirty miles due east of Halifax, Nova Scotia. No positive identification has been made so far, but it seems possible that the wreckage is that of a supercargo space ship——

MARK: That must be the thing Taylor picked up on his radar. That's why he couldn't hold it—it was falling.— Lowell! Battle wagon. It must be a battle wagon. They've knocked down a battle wagon. Find out— find out from Crandall——

LOWELL: Get Ismay, quick.

JORDAN: Yes, sir.

MARK: I—I—I——

"Switch it off," Lowell said.

Neil switched the machine off, his nerves throbbing.

"He recovered pretty fast," Lowell said. "Nothing for you to be alarmed about, Neil."

"He's only just hanging onto life," Neil said.

"Hanging on! No, sir! He's gripping it with both hands," Lowell said, and began to laugh. "For a man who sees humanity the way he does, he's certainly in no hurry to quit. Whereas I feel optimistic about the human race, I'll defend it to the last ditch, but look at me . . ." He sat down heavily in the armchair. "I'm awfully tired, Neil. I'm awfully tired and dispirited."

"Can I get you something, sir?"

"No. I'll be all right." He smiled bitterly. "At least, I learned something from that conversation with Mark."

"What was that, sir?"

"We don't know what the Ampiti will do next."

7

AT TEN o'clock that evening Dr. Werner made his global broadcast. He said nothing new, and he made no reference to battle wagons. His speech, in effect, was mild and unalarming, merely stating that the observatory on New Panama had picked up a number of flying objects (number unspecified), and so had Platform Alpha; that InterCos was naturally keeping an eye on these visitors but had no definite information about them so far. This, he said, was a remarkable discovery, of the greatest scientific interest since it presumably confirmed the theory that life existed outside our own planet. There was no reason to be afraid of these so-far unidentified visitors, he pointed out; for even though Earth had cur-tailed the production of armaments, we still possessed certain defenses which were so powerful, so terrifying, that no attack against us was possible, no enemy could survive our counterattack. It was not correct at present, he stated, to term these visitors as hostile since they had not in any way declared their intentions; he simply re-ferred to our impenetrable defenses in order to allay any nervousness which might be felt in certain quarters. For a few minutes he dwelt on the phenomenon of visitors entering our space zones, treating it as a matter of pro-found scientific-philosophical value, which was bound to affect and enlarge our concept of the Universe; and for a few minutes he dwelt on the role of InterCos, we, the instruments of a purpose; and for a few minutes he touched lightly on the subject of defenses, and that was all. An admirable speech, Neil thought, listening to it with SecState Lowell. Authoritative, yet full of charm.

"Let's see what he left out," Lowell said. "No reference to the Committee of Five, no reference to taking over as Supreme Commander. Nothing about closing the Sahara and Lake Baikal workshops, nothing about this crash off Halifax. What else?"

"He didn't refer to that latest bulletin we received this afternoon," Neil said. *"Specific contact has been made with the craft which entered our space zones. We've heard nothing more about it."*

"He's covering up," Lowell said gloomily. "A bad sign."

The broadcast to the Ampiti was not for global consumption. It was carried at eleven-thirty on the red circuit, the internal circuit at InterCos restricted to officials no lower than aides and the heads of certain key departments. This speech was delivered very slowly, with extreme clarity, and with deep feeling; it sounded like a wise, dignified, but somewhat indignant headmaster addressing a classroom of surly children. Again, Dr. Werner said nothing new. He made no reference to battle wagons. His theme was brotherhood, co-operation, peace. He alluded only in passing to certain weapons which had made warfare impossible on Earth because they were so powerful, so terrifying, that no defense against them was possible. Now, he stated, Earth held firmly to one purpose, of which InterCos was the instrument: the glorious purpose of universal friendship, the flowering of universal culture, the abolition of all cosmic frontiers so that the benefits of research and discovery should be available to all the inhabitants of the Cosmos. The denial of such benefits to any group within the Cosmos, he declared, would be a grave moral injustice. He proposed high-level conversations. He stated that Earth would be listening, as it had always listened, for evidence of the Ampiti's intentions. Earth was listening now not only with its ears but with its heart also.

A splendid speech. Neil thought. It would no doubt be reprinted verbatim in the InterCos magazine, which was entitled *Our Universe* and subtitled *Man's Empire in Space*. This subtitle might have to be changed for the next issue, however.

SecState Lowell looked sad and tired. He made no comment on the Supreme Commander's remarks. He went to bed almost at once.

Neil lay awake for a long time. Sleep did not come easily tonight. He recalled, with shock, with astonishment, that several hours ago he had been with Libby in this very building, and that something of paramount importance had taken place—a declaration of mutual affection. He was a little puzzled because, in a sense, he had expressed more than affection, he had felt more than affection, more than fondness and more than physical longing. He wanted her (surprisingly) not near him, here, but away from him, several hundred miles away. Out of the city. He remembered how when he was speaking to her about this he had felt a trembling of concern for her, a terror that some mishap might overtake her; he had felt a wild, emotional determination to protect her at any cost to himself. Did the parapsychologists have a name for feelings of this kind?

He thought, too, of Mark, and Lowell, and the Committee of Five balanced so uneasily on the fulcrum of Dhevu: Balatov, Hsuen on one side, Crandall, Vernon on the other. The rulers of the world. As he fell asleep he vaguely wondered if the Ampiti ever engaged in political revels of this kind, if the Ampiti had their Hsuens and Balatovs, if the Ampiti ever experienced affection that was so deeply tinged with fear.

The aide to the Turkish Minister woke him at three o'clock in the morning with a message that the Turkish Minister sent his deepest regrets but begged to confer with the American Minister on a matter of the highest importance and the greatest secrecy. It was unfortunately impossible for the Turkish Minister to leave his office at the moment: would it therefore be asking too much for the honorable American Minister to come there, and immediately?

"What's the trouble?" Neil asked in a protective growl.

The aide answered nervously. It was something concerning the present crisis, extremely serious. The manner in which the man spoke was alarming.

Neil woke SecState Lowell, found his slippers, helped him into a robe, and accompanied him to the offices of the Turkish Delegation. He waited in the anteroom with the Turkish aide, and they chatted in an ambiguously diplomatic way about the delights of water polo, about fishing in the Carpathians, the charming parties given by the wife of the French Minister. They had plenty of time to converse. SecState Lowell did not reappear for three-quarters of an hour.

In the corridor Lowell said in a hard voice, "We'd better see Mark."

"Sir," Neil said wildly, "he's probably asleep. He didn't get any sleep last night."

"Neither did I," Lowell snapped. They returned to the Delegation suite, and Lowell went angrily to his room and slammed the door. The news passed on by the Turkish Minister had upset him badly; and Neil waited outside.

Lowell called a moment later, "Are you there, Neil?"

Neil went in. He was sitting on his bed, a tired, dejected, gray old man.

"What has happened, sir?"

"Kemel read me some code messages that have just come in from Istanbul," Lowell began; then stopped, as if he could not bring himself to say any more.

"About the Ampiti?"

Lowell went on with an effort, "In a way. Istanbul has learned from its agents that both the Sahara and Lake Baikal workshops have been reactivated. They're very active. It appears that preparations are being made to launch the final Beta sections tonight." He glanced at his watch. "They may, in fact, have been fired already."

"But the Council of Ministers hasn't approved——"

"The Supreme Commander," Lowell said grimly, "has full powers to take such action without approval by the Council of Ministers. The Supreme Commander, evidently, can do more or less what he pleases from this time on, and we can't even protest." His mouth tightened. "I suppose you're right. Mark can wait to hear this after he's had his breakfast.—Go to bed, Neil. You need sleep, too."

"I'll stay here with you, sir——"

"What's the use?" Lowell said. "What can we do? Go to bed."

At five o'clock Neil woke again. He had been sleeping heavily, but some noise had penetrated his consciousness —a whistle?—a thump like a distant explosion?

He could not tell.

He went to sleep again. The noise was not repeated.

He was up again at seven, and in the Delegation office soon after eight; and for some time he was very busy. SecState Lowell had requested that several advisors be sent from Washington, and they had arrived promptly: a senior State Department official named Hooper, and two ranking officers of the Air Force and the Navy, General Kirkland and Admiral Gould. Neither had ever heard a shot fired in anger. The British had also asked for similar assistance; so had the Canadian and Australian Ministers. At eleven o'clock a mass briefing session was held for the benefit of these new arrivals. Lowell gave a carefully worded summary of the situation, omitting any reference to the report from Istanbul. Berkeley spoke, too. He said, with unusual bluntness, "SecState Lowell has informed you of events up to the present moment, but only insofar as we know of them from confirmed reports. You are all men of wide experience: you realize how in a time of stress rumors of every sort are apt to get into circulation, and I can assure you that such rumors are plentiful here today, some of them exceedingly alarming. You will also realize that questions of policy are now to all intents and purposes out of our hands, as are all questions of strategy. These matters rest entirely with the Supreme Commander and the Committee of Five. If there is a war (and there may be a war going on this minute) it will be conducted from a locked room—to which we have no access—against an enemy we cannot see. The Council of Ministers will function as a sort of watchdog, of which the members here form only the rump. It will be your function, gentlemen, to advise us when we should, or should not, wag our tail. I am afraid that we will be powerless to do more than that."

The British naval officer rose. "Will the restriction on the use of f-materials remain in force?"

Berkeley answered, "That's for the Supreme Commander to decide. He may consult the Council of Ministers, since the decision is of such a grave nature; on the other hand, he is not bound to do so."

General Kirkland asked, "What about the use of battle wagons?"

Lowell said, "We have no information of a definite nature."

Kirkland pondered the answer. The phrasing was significant, and he sat back, staring at Lowell.

Admiral Gould said, "Mr. Secretary, you alluded to a bulletin about contact being established with the Ampiti. Could you explain this?"

Lowell said, "We are ourselves still awaiting an explanation. My private feeling is that we will not receive any. One of our experts has advanced the theory that this alleged 'contact' now is lying wrecked off the coast of Nova Scotia."

Kirkland said sharply, "A battle wagon?"

"We don't know, General."

"Mr. Secretary," Kirkland said, "I'm sorry to pursue this subject, but I'd like to point out that it's vitally important for us to know. Have battle wagons gone into action? Has one been brought down? How? What weapons are the Ampiti using? This is very serious, sir."

"We realize that it's serious," Lowell replied. "Unfortunately, we can't do a thing about it."

"But——"

"That's the situation, General."

The British military advisor asked, "Is it contemplated, sir, to alert the public to the present danger?"

Berkeley answered, "Not as far as we've been in-formed."

"May I suggest that we should do so without delay? The public should be instructed to report landings, form defense units——"

Berkeley said, "That's a decision for the Committee of Five."

"But, sir——"

"Both SecState Lowell and I pointed this out in our opening remarks. We are the servants of InterCos. Dr. Werner is our Supreme Commander and the Committee of Five is our High Command. Our duty is to wait for instructions."

The discussion was ended abruptly by a message from the acting President, requesting the Ministers to assemble in the Council Chamber at noon precisely. Ministers' advisors and their aides, the acting President said, were also permitted to attend.

SecState Lowell said sourly, "That sounds like trouble."

Berkeley said in sudden bewilderment, "How the dickens did we get into this mess?"

The acting President was a Swiss who looked in some ways strangely like Dr. Werner. He was tall, thin, with a narrow face and white hair; but he was nervous as he stood on the podium. He lacked Werner's vitality, the assurance that could stir an audience.

He said, adjusting his spectacles, "I must apologize for calling this meeting at such short notice. I did so only because of a bulletin which I received at eleven twenty-five, which I felt I should deliver to you personally." He looked around the Chamber, as if he expected immedi-ate opposition, and then hastily began to read from a red folder.

"At the request of the Supreme Commander, the fol-lowing information is passed to the Council of Ministers:

"Last night, after his global broadcast, the Supreme Commander made a special space broadcast which was subsequently rebroadcast in twenty-six languages, ap-pealing to the craft which have entered our space zones for peaceful co-operation and universal friendship, and proposing high-level conferences to achieve these ends.

"At five o'clock this morning an explosion was heard in New Jersey, on the outskirts of Jersey City. Police who investigated the occurrence have since reported that the explosion was evidently caused by an accumulation of gases in underground public utility conduits.

"It has been learned, however, that there have been similar explosions in or near London, Paris, Prague, Budapest, Leningrad, Capetown, Madras, Shanghai, and several other cities.

"In all cases, the explosions occurred at approximately the same time. No unduly serious results have been reported. In Shanghai, where the explosion demolished several buildings in a crowded residential district, twenty-five bodies have so far been recovered. In London there were two fatalities. There were no fatalities in New Jersey.

"These incidents may have been an attempt at widespread sabotage; but a possibility exists that they represent a deliberate attack by hostile forces. In this connection it is important to repeat that the damage done in each case was relatively small and is in no way comparable to the severe damage which could be inflicted even by mid-twentieth-century weapons or the infinitely greater damage which could be inflicted by later weapons controlled by InterCos.

"Bearing in mind that Earth may have been subjected to hostile attack, the Supreme Commander nevertheless urges that all Ministers should exercise calmness and restraint, in the hope that further acts of aggression may be averted. A new mass-language space broadcast is now being prepared, appealing in stronger and more concrete terms for friendly negotiation in the interests of universal peace, stressing our horror at unprovoked invasion and unprovoked attack. In this new broadcast it has been thought advisable to refrain from any mention of retaliation; but future broadcasts will, if necessary, carry the warning that Earth possesses all means to exterminate even the largest invading fleet at a single blow.

"For defensive purposes the Supreme Commander has ordered the reactivation of the InterCos installations at Sahara and Lake Baikal; and, to protect the vital sections of the Beta Complex which were already positioned on the firing ramps, these have now been launched.

"Certain other defense measures have been initiated, and these will be announced in later bulletins. The advisability of appointing a Director of Public Safety is now being considered.

"The Supreme Commander regrets to announce that a large defense craft, undergoing tests, failed in flight and crashed in the North Atlantic Ocean. There were no survivors."

The Ministers sat in silence; and the acting President took off his spectacles, wiped them in a handkerchief, and held them up to peer through them at the dome of the Council Chamber.

SecState Lowell rose and said, "Mr. President."

The acting President put his spectacles on hurriedly and said, "The Chair recognizes the honorable Minister Plenipotentiary from the United States."

Lowell said, "I request the following information: at what time did the Supreme Commander order the reactivation of the Sahara and Lake Baikal installations?"

"The time?"

"I ask with special reason, Mr. President. Was the reactivation ordered before or after five o'clock this morning?"

"I am afraid," the acting President said with a vague smile, "that I have no information on that matter beyond what is contained in the bulletin." Somebody on the other side of the Chamber stood up, and he said, "The Chair recognizes——"

Lowell said loudly, "Mr. President, I have not yet yielded the floor. This is a matter of the utmost gravity. I have information that the reactivation was ordered before five o'clock this morning, that it was ordered in fact early last evening——"

"Mr. Lowell, I regret that I have no way of confirming or denying your statement."

"I beg your permission, Mr. President, to complete my statement. This statement is important. I claim that the sequence of events here is vital in judging who is guilty of aggression. If, as I have good reason to believe, the reactivation of the workshops was ordered early last night, along with other military measures, then it would be possible to construe these acts not as defensive but as warlike in intent. In consequence, the mysterious explosions referred to might well be retaliatory——"

A bell rang out, and Lowell stopped talking at once.

"Mr. Lowell," the acting President said sternly, "your statement is merely a series of assumptions which could cause prolonged debate, without any factual basis for such debate. I must therefore ask you kindly to be seated."

Lowell said in a calm voice, "Yes, Mr. President."

Locke, the New Zealander, was standing. "Mr. President."

The acting President looked around the Chamber, and then reluctantly recognized him.

"Mr. President," Locke said, "I request that a message be sent to the Supreme Commander, asking at what time the reactivation of the workshops was ordered."

"I fail to see the purpose of this request, Mr. Locke."

"The purpose is simple, sir. It is to discover if possible whether the Supreme Commander is ordering military action at the same time that he is assuring the Ampiti of his peaceful intentions."

The Russian deputy Minister shouted, "Rubbish!"

Madame Ai-Wen-Tai, deputizing for the lord Hsuen, stood up and said something which could not be heard over the uproar.

The bell clanged again.

The acting President cried, "I ask for silence! The Ministers will kindly restrain themselves!"

The Chamber became quite.

"The Chair recognizes the honorable Minister Plenipotentiary from the Republic of China."

She was old and very frail, and her voice was so low that Neil had to turn and watch her lips as she spoke.

"Mr. President, I rise with sorrow, hearing the noble Ministers fighting among themselves so bitterly and so soon. Mr. President, inevitably there have been differences between us in the past. That is only human. But now we are faced with a common threat to our security, and it is tragic to feel that we are divided. There should be no place now for strife in our midst. We should be single-minded, a single-body, a single heart. Perhaps we are all overtired and overstrained. Perhaps we should retire for a few hours to recompose ourselves, so that when we reconvene we shall be able to discuss these matters without rancor. I propose, Mr. President, a recess until three o'clock."

The Venezuelan Minister rose to second her; but as he stood up, very distinctly from somewhere to the east of the Council Chamber—quite far to the east—there were two separate thuds and two separate trials of sound like thunder going from the earth to the sky. Automatically, Neil looked at his watch. The time was twelve fifty-five; but this was not really significant. He heard the bell ring to close the meeting, and he followed SecState Lowell out of the Council Chamber. General Kirkland smiled at him as if to say, *Did you hear it?* and he smiled palely in return; but in his mind there was only one thought, one name, Libby.

Kirkland said in a kindly way to Mark, "I'd like to get a few ideas straight, with your help. This is all new to me, you know, Professor. I've only been at it a few hours."

The fat man was desperately tired. The flesh was sagging on the moon face; the skin looked waxy, bloodless, gray-white. He said, "Sit down, sir. Make yourself comfortable. All of you. Learn to relax, you'll live longer."

They ranged themselves in a circle around him: Kirkland, Admiral Gould, Hooper, Lowell, and Neil. Mark looked from one to the other, and mumbled something under his breath.

121

"Professor?" Kirkland insisted. He was about forty-five years old, trim, distinguished, very soldierly in his Army uniform.

Gould said in a loud voice, "I'm interested in this green stuff. This green stuff on the Hudson. Burning stuff. It's dangerous. What about that, Professor?"

"I'm interested in it, too," Mark said. "But let's not go so fast, because I want to tell you something first." He looked from Gould to Kirkland. "I've already told Lowell. It must be very exciting for you boys to be in a war at last, but don't go pressing any buttons. Don't send up any interceptors."

"I know that," Kirkland said pleasantly. He was obviously sorry for the sick man and not upset by his sour manner. "I'd just like to think aloud for a minute or so, and get your reactions. For example, I'm thinking about these two explosions in Forest Hills——"

"Keep thinking, General," Mark croaked. "I'm on your wave length."

Kirkland went on without any change in his voice: "The police report that the craters are about thirty feet deep, only about fifteen feet wide. We can get our experts to figure out the story from that data—the type of missile, how it hit, and so on; but what puzzles me is this: it's a small crater. The missile that makes craters this size is a small missile."

"Thank your lucky stars," Mark said harshly.

"Now," Kirkland continued, 'here are these Ampiti. They move through space at an incredible rate. They must have techniques that are infinitely superior to ours. They've presumably started hostilities. And yet this is apparently the best that they can do—drill a couple of puny holes in the ground, miles away from any worthwhile target. It doesn't make sense."

Mark leered at him. "Makes you unhappy, eh? You'd be a lot happier if they dropped a couple of Type 12 hydrogen bombs?"

"No," Kirkland said, smiling. "I can't understand it, that's all."

"I told Lowell last night," Mark said. "Don't expect

the Ampiti to think the way you think. I told him, the only thing you can predict about them is that they're unpredictable.—Didn't I tell you that, Mr. Secretary?" He shouted the question.

"You did, Mark. I have the tape to prove it."

"Keep that tape," Mark said. "It might turn out to be my last will and testament."

Gould, drier and older than Kirkland, said, "Professor, do you think that's the best these characters can do? Drop a couple of firecrackers? It's a significant point."

"I wouldn't know, sir. I'm not a mind reader. But the General here put it clearly—the Ampiti came a long way fast, they have better techniques than ours, and if they mean business why haven't they converted Manhattan into gaseous vapor by now?—Well, why haven't they?"

"Waiting for InterCos to negotiate?" Gould suggested.

"InterCos has already offered to negotiate," Mark snapped. "Apparently the Ampiti weren't impressed."

Hooper, the new man from the State Department, said with a little cough, "We shouldn't forget that two of—er—these *things* were also dropped on London."

"Paris," Kirkland added. "Prague, Leningrad, Capetown, Chicago, all the rest. And all at the same time, and all the same type of small missile. Any suggestions, Professor?"

"I can't think Ampiti thoughts," Mark said. "The best I can do is throw out the idea that they're using these small ones (a) because they don't *have* any big ones or (b) because they prefer not to *use* big ones. Does that help you?"

Kirkland laughed. "Not very much."

Gould burst in. "Let's get down to practical matters. What about this stuff they found in the Hudson early today? This green stuff that grows?"

"That?" Mark said. "The burning fungus? That's really cute, isn't it?"

The captain of one of the ferries had reported the green fungus. A small sailboat had been caught in a patch of it that was floating on the surface, a patch about twenty feet square; and the skipper of this sailboat was signaling for help because, for some inexplicable reason, his craft was burning at the water line. As the ferry approached, the sailboat began to sink; its skipper jumped, but could not clear the fungus. He screamed as he floundered in it, went under and came up screaming again, and then disappeared. It was called fungus already because when the river police came to investigate there was more of the smelly, green, mossy stuff, about forty square feet, and the edges of it could be seen wavering further and further outward. A policeman who dropped a metal pail into it in a laudable attempt to collect some for analysis, had the strange experience of seeing the side of the pail smolder and dribble away like hot grease. It had a vile smell.

"Phosphorus?" Admiral Gould asked.

Mark said curtly, "Phosphorus would have been identified by now. It must be something else. Some new substance."

"We'll have to stop it," Gould said. "It could be a menace to shipping. We *must* stop it."

"Sure, sure. An excellent suggestion."

Gould lost his temper. "Now look here, Dr. Harrison. It's all very fine for you to sit there and be amusing. But this isn't amusing. It's serious. I came in here because I was told you were our big expert and I hoped I'd hear some sense about the situation. But it looks to me as if we're just wasting our time."

Mark said, "Ask Lowell. Mr. Secretary, isn't it a fact that I've been warning you for the best part of a year that there was going to be trouble? Nobody would listen. Here it is. *Trouble.* So don't come to me and tell me I'm being funny. You people asked for trouble and now you've got it, all of you. And from what I can see it's going to be big trouble, plenty trouble, and you're going to have to face it to the bitter end, unless you find your Benedict Arnold and get him to intercede on your account."

Lowell said, "All right, Mark. Take it easy, take it easy."

Mark swung round in rage. "The day cometh, my

friend, the day cometh, as the book prophesied. Did you think you could get away with treachery for ever?"

"I've never tried to get away with treachery," Lowell said. He blinked at the fat man in mild reproof, and Mark's rage turned to surliness. Then Lowell asked, "What are the Voices doing now? Has there been any change?"

Mark did not answer for a moment. "No. Same gabble. Same distance. Nothing new."

Lowell walked over to him and put a hand on his shoulder. "I want you to rest. Be sensible. We'll be needing you badly. Rest as much as you can."

Mark said shrilly, "Get out of here, Mr. Secretary, before I have you thrown out."

Lowell chuckled. He said to the other men, "Let's go."

Mark said, "Neil, stay here. I want to talk to you."

Bernie Ismay came hurrying into the room as soon as it was clear and said accusingly to Neil, "I'll give you one minute. He's exhausted. If he doesn't get some sleep I refuse to be responsible for the consequences."

"I'm being persecuted," Mark yelled. "I'm being hounded on all sides——"

"Be quiet," Ismay said. "Act your age. And don't try that stuff with me. It won't work.—Just one minute, Neil." He walked out, looking pointedly at his wrist watch.

Mark laughed weakly and his enormous body seemed to sag. "Good old Bernie. He's doing his best. Trying to keep me going for another six months."

Neil's mouth became dry. "Longer than that, Mark."

"Not a hope," Mark said. His head drooped with fatigue. "Three months, if I'm lucky. Less.—I've been meaning to ask you: where's Libby?"

"At her apartment."

"I guessed as much," Mark said. His voice rose with urgency. "It isn't too late yet. Talk her into leaving town, make her realize——"

"I tried, Mark. She won't go."

The words were a mumble. "Shame. What a shame.

Never had a chance to be happy. Too bad, too bad.—
You know what's happening? We're through.—Poor Libby. Poor Evelyn. Poor little human race. Never had a
chance."

He was so weak that Neil said, "Why don't you sleep
for a while? I'll come in and see you later."

"No. No. Stay.—Who's this fellow Hart von—von——"

"Von Horstmann? Why?"

"Called me several times. Wants to come in and see
me. Bernie told him, no. Impossible to see me."

Neil said, "He's Werner's aide. He probably wants to
pick your brains."

"Poor brains.—Neil, I didn't think they'd be so brutal,
so intolerant. I thought they'd be kinder, honestly I did."

"Who?"

"The Ampiti. These little missiles, this green fungus
stuff. Honest, Neil, I thought they'd be . . . in my heart,
I thought they'd be . . . understanding. I thought they'd
have all the qualities we don't have. Godlike. You know,
stern but with living kindness. I didn't think they'd
throw anything like this green stuff at us. And those
little missiles, little needles."

Neil said, "I don't understand you."

Bernie Ismay had returned, and was standing at the
door.

"Man," Mark said with a sigh. "Little homo sapiens.
You can't help feeling sorry for the little fellow . . . poor
little fellow. Achieved so much. Such fine things, marvelous things, surprising things. Music, poetry, calculus,
fission——Awful proud of him, sometimes. Why did he
have to get so tricky—lying, cheating, thieving, destroy-
ing? Why couldn't he stay good and decent, creative?
Original sin, eh? And then, stupid little chap, why did he
have to get up there and defy the Universe? Eh?—We're
all in this together, Neil, we're all responsible, every man
jack of us. Glorious dreams. Space. Man's empire. We
all took part in it. But someone should have said, No,
little people, not until you've cleansed your soiled little
souls and washed out your dirty little hearts; until then
you'd better stay right where you are——But, believe me,

Neil, I didn't expect the Ampiti to be so tough. So ruthless. That green stuff——" His voice petered out. The great swollen hands twitched and then hung down loosely; the sunken eyes were closed.

Bernie Ismay said, "Leave him now, Neil."

Mark began to speak again, like an exhausted man talking in his sleep. "Spreads," he said. "Spreads. Burns. Green. Moss, fungus, organic . . . non-organic? What is it?—Spreads, burns, green-moss-fungus?-organic-non-organic, spreadsburnsgreenmoss, spreadsburnsgreenmoss . . . spreads. Burns. Yes. Spreads, burns, yes, I see. Completes the circuit. That's right. As long as the switch is pressed, current flows from negative to positive, yes, green stuff grows, yes, continues to grow, yes, fungus burns. But only while switch is pressed. Yes. I see."

Neil whispered to Ismay, "What's he saying?"

"I don't know. It doesn't make any sense to me. He's been doing this a lot recently. I'll give him some dope tonight, make sure he gets plenty of sleep."

Neil looked at the fat man in pity. Then he said to Ismay, "Have you heard that Evelyn has stayed in town? She didn't go to New Hampshire."

Ismay nodded. "I've spoken to her. I'm glad. I can call her any time it's necessary. It isn't going to be long now."

Mark had begun to snore heavily.

"How long?" Neil asked.

"Days I'm afraid. Ten. Nine. Maybe less."

"I'm sorry he had to be brought here."

"So am I," Ismay said. "But *he* isn't. He's having the time of his life. Up to his eyes in everything. Bossing Lowell around, and the rest of them." He laughed angrily. "I've grown awfully fond of him. I'm going to miss him like mad."

Neil called Libby a few minutes before the Council of Ministers reconvened. When she answered she was holding her scaly poodle in her arms.

"Neil," she said. "Neil.—Matilda, look! Here's Neil

at last!" The dog barked in a puzzled way at the image on the screen, and then Libby put it down on a chair.

"How are you?" Neil asked.

"I'm fine, Neil. Do you know what I'm doing?"

"What?"

"Waiting. Just waiting. Waiting for you to come to see me."

He said unhappily, "Libby, I can't get over today."

"Oh, Neil!" She could not hide her disappointment.

"I'm sorry. I can't tell you how sorry. But it's a madhouse here."

"Of course," she said. "I understand." And then she said in quick concern, her eyes meeting his almost as if she were present in the room, "Please take care of yourself. You're looking tired. Don't work too hard——" She stopped, afraid of her own emotion, and he saw her make an effort to talk of something else. She asked, "Is Mark well?"

"I just saw him. He's feeling pretty good."

"I talked to Evelyn this morning. I asked her to come and stay here with me. She said, No, she had to stay put in case Mark needed her. Then she asked me to come and stay with her, and I said, No, I had to stay put in case——"

"In case what?"

"For you," Libby said.

He could not speak.

"Please come as soon as you can, Neil. I'm very lonesome for you, my dear."

"I promise," he said. "Tomorrow. Tomorrow, for sure."

"I hate to worry you," she cried. "Forgive me. I've never felt, never acted this way before."

"It's all new to me, too. Please take care of yourself."

She smiled tearfully. "Yes. Until tomorrow. I hope I can wait until tomorrow."

He thought, *Craters thirty feet deep, only fifteen feet wide. Burning green fungus that spreads.* He was so frightened that he was unable to go on speaking to her.

He said, "Good-by," and switched off, his entire body trembling as if he had suddenly been struck by plague.

What had General Kirkland called them? *A couple of puny holes in the ground.*

Puny, Neil thought. *That's good. Nothing to worry about. They're just puny. Miles from any worth-while target, too. That's very good.*

As soon as the acting President opened the meeting SecState Lowell rose again to demand information about the time of the reactivation of the two workshops. But Neil could sense—and in all probability the other Ministers sensed it also—that there was no real urgency, no real force in Lowell's speech. There were other matters now, far more serious, far more puzzling, on which the Ministers restlessly awaited information. The green fungus. The two bombs that had fallen in Forest Hills, and on London, Paris, Prague, Capetown, and the rest.

But the acting President had an answer ready for Lowell, and he produced it with a flourish, like a conjurer producing a rabbit from a hat. He said, adjusting his glasses, "There has been a personal message from the Supreme Commander which I think fully answers the question put by the honorable Minister. I have it here." He opened another of his folders and began to read: "From the Supreme Commander, Global Headquarters. The following facts (classified, Secret, Code Red) are made available to the Council of Ministers for policy reasons:

"*One:* The large defense craft, previously announced as lost over the North Atlantic Ocean during tests, crashed shortly before noon yesterday.

"*Two:* Some evidence was immediately available that this crash was not due to accidental causes.

"*Three:* The Committee of Five, the Supreme Commander concurring, thereupon decided on the following action:

(a) reactivation of certain InterCos installations which earlier had been closed.

(b) dispatch of three large defense craft to guard our space zones from hostile attack.

"Four: One of the defense craft referred to in 3 (b) subsequently reported contact with the craft that have entered our space areas, but has not been heard of since. The other two defense craft are maintaining their allotted position.

"Five: The most earnest efforts are being continued to avoid any open clash, and the Supreme Commander has made a third space broadcast in twenty-six languages stating our peaceful intentions and requesting immediate negotiations."

The acting President put the folder down. "Signed," he said mildly, "by the Supreme Comander over the seal of the Committee of Five."

Lowell cried, "Mr. President, I most humbly and respectfully beg to point out that this document not only confirms my argument, but most significantly relates it to happenings several hours earlier. I beg to point out that while the Supreme Commander is broadcasting appeals for peaceful negotiations he is at the same time sending defense craft into the air; and we all know what these defense craft are. Now it seems that we have lost not one but two of these defense craft, presumably by action of the Ampiti. But are we sure who is the aggressor? We should be clear about this——"

A dozen Ministers were on their feet, shouting, waving, clamoring to be heard. The Presidential bell clanged again and again, until sullenly and reluctantly the Ministers became quiet.

The acting President said in great agitation, "Unless the Chamber conducts itself in a more seemly manner I shall be forced to declare this meeting adjourned."

"Adjourn!" the Polish Minister shouted. "Adjourn!"

The cry was taken up around the great hall, and was met by an opposing cry of "No, no! No, no!" Under the stress of powerful emotion the Spanish and Portuguese Ministers suddenly chose this moment to resume their private quarrels by violently grappling with each other, the Chilean and Peruvian Ministers joined in the fracas, the Brazilian Minister received a bloody nose trying to separate them, and to everybody's astonishment Dhevu's sister fainted.

Pale but relieved, the acting President rang his bell three times, quoted an appropriate rule that applied to disorder in the Chamber, and declared the meeting adjourned until further notice.

8

CURIOUSLY, there was no widespread public alarm over the two explosions in Forest Hills. Only one tele-news commentator was alert enough to associate these ex-plosions with that reported earlier from New Jersey; and he, with great indignation, called for the ouster of the men responsible for national sewage policy, those old fuddy-duddies (he said) who sat in plush offices in Wash-ington and didn't give a hoot about the menace of anti-quated sewers. He prophesied, moreover, that the ex-plosions would continue until the Administration woke up and took the bull by the horns to end this national disgrace. He demanded a new sewage system and he de-manded it now.

Neither—until several hours afterward—was there any large-scale reaction to Dr. Werner's broadcast. Dr. Wer-ner was familiar to tele audiences. It was part of his policy to keep the peoples of the world informed about Inter-Cos and its magnificent purpose, and he did this by appearing frequently in fireside chats and, more form-ally, in a "State of InterCos" message at the end of each year. This latest broadcast was certainly news; but there had been thousands of reports for more than a century of unidentified flying objects entering Earth's space zones, and it seemed to many people that he was merely confirming a known fact which for some bureaucratic reason had never officially been confirmed before. A large number of citizens went around the next morning saying triumphantly, "I told you so." A smaller number stubbornly maintained that Dr. Werner was only looking for publicity and argued—like a popular British diplomat—about space dust and refraction.

But by the middle of the afternoon the Information Office attached to the American Delegation at InterCos began to be swamped with calls. People all over the United States went to their telesets with questions that indicated mounting interest. Was it true that there were thirty-five thousand of these ships from outer space? Was it true that some had landed in Wisconsin, Nebraska, Arkansas, the Merritt Parkway? Was it true that they were piloted by midgets eighteen inches tall who could only live on human blood? A lady from Pennsylvania called to say that a space ship was hovering at that very moment over her house, and what should she do to get rid of it? Another lady called from Buffalo to say she had seen something with six legs in her back yard—she was sure it had six legs—and she wanted protection.

Questions of this sort were to be expected. There were similar calls whenever InterCos announced any new development. Nervous or excitable or foolish people always reacted by calling with idiotic statements and idiotic suggestions. But gradually the character of the calls changed. Neil, kept informed by the officer in charge of the Information Office, had the impression that more and more people had begun to examine Dr. Werner's statement with care; they were wondering precisely what it meant and precisely what had motivated it. People were asking questions that had a sharper appreciation of the situation; and it was often difficult to satisfy them with oblique answers.

At five o'clock the managing editor of one of the leading news agencies called, a man, named Jerre Hadfield. His call was put through to Neil.

Hadfield said, "I want to speak to SecState Lowell."

"Sorry, Jerre. He's in conference."

"Crandall, then."

"I'm very sorry. Crandall isn't available."

On the telescreen Hadfield looked grim. "I want a

statement, Neil, and I want it from a top source. How about you?"

"What's on your mind, Jerre?"

"Werner's broadcast last night. Also the events that have followed since."

Neil said carefully, "I'm not sure what you mean. What events?"

"Let's not beat about the bush. We've been adding up some facts. There was an explosion in Jersey City this morning. Strangely enough, our correspondents reported explosions in other places, London, Paris, Shanghai, about the same time—nothing important enough for a big story, merely brief news items. We've just been going over them, and it seems like a curious coincidence that there should be so many sewers blowing up at the same hour. Still, it could be. However, around one o'clock today there were two explosions in Forest Hills, and our men have been sending in reports of two in London, two in Paris, two in Chicago, two in Prague, two in Shanghai, et cetera, et cetera. Also at the same time.— Any comment?"

"No," Neil said.

Hadfield went on in the same grim way, "There's also this green stuff on the Hudson. We can't figure that out. It's killed a couple of people who happened to come into contact with it. First reports were that it was some chemical that had been accidentally discharged by a tanker. Now we hear it's floating around the Thames and the Seine, it's done a lot of damage to shipping in Hong Kong, it's been noticed in a dozen other places. Queer stuff. Nobody knows exactly what it is. Seems to grow. Spreads pretty fast.—Any comment on that?"

"No," Neil said. "Sorry."

"All right," Hadfield said. "Here's another thing. Are you getting many calls from the public?"

"A few."

"Our lines have been tied up for three hours. And I want to tell you something. It isn't the usual lunatic fringe. People sound as if they're worried. For example,

134

a lot of our callers are asking, have we mobilized our defense forces, and if not why not.—Have we?"

"Not to my knowledge."

"Have we recommissioned our force of battle wagons?"

"I couldn't say."

"Are there any plans for organizing the public in civil defense units, observer units, or anything of that kind?"

"Sorry, Jerre, I couldn't tell you."

Hadfield said, "Have the mighty Lords of InterCos made up their great minds yet about these so-called visitors? Do we consider them hostile or not hostile?"

"I don't know."

"That's fine," Hadfield said. "That's dandy. You're a splendid diplomat, and a credit to the State Department, Neil, and I've always considered you a good friend. But here's what I'm going to do. I'm going to leave those questions in your lap, and I'm going to switch off now, but I'm going to keep this circuit open. And I want answers to those questions in fifteen minutes, or else. If this is an emergency the public ought to know about it now. They ought to have the facts, and they ought to have the facts straight. Understand?"

"I understand," Neil said "I'll call you in fifteen minutes."

He switched off and went into Crandall's office to see SecState Lowell.

Lowell listened to Neil's account of the conversation and said, "It was inevitable. Hadfield isn't a fool, and there are plenty of people just as shrewd as he is. They're putting two and two together and coming up with an answer that's a lot more than four. We can't stall them much longer. Some statement will have to be made; but we ourselves can't make it without authorization from the Supreme Commander."

Neil said angrily, "The Supreme Commander had better act fast or there's going to be trouble."

"Call von Horstmann," Lowell said. "Find out from him whether any statement is being issued in the next hour. If not, I'll speak to Hadfield personally."

"Will you give him the facts?"

Lowell said, "I don't know yet." He smiled. "I'll now go into executive session with my conscience and try to figure that out."

"Will you tell him we've lost two battle wagons already?"

Lowell said, "I doubt if my conscience would go so far as to disclose military secrets."

"Mr. Secretary," Neil said, "when is a secret secret? The Ampiti presumably know they've destroyed two battle wagons. Who are we trying to keep the information from?"

"I'm an old fox," Lowell said. "Don't try to trip me with leading questions."

Neil returned to his desk and called Hart on the internal teleset.

Hart smiled cheerfully when Neil finished talking. He said, "Sure, Neil, I know. I've had a dozen messages from Ministers, all the same story. Editors, commentators, asking the same things."

"Well," Neil demanded, "what can I tell Hadfield?"

"At this moment, nothing."

"Hart, we can't go on like this."

"The only news I can give you is that the Supreme Commander is contemplating another global broadcast at nine o'clock tonight."

"*Contemplating!*"

"Yes. I will let you know about it as soon as I hear definitely.—How is your brother?"

"Fine," Neil said, and switched off in anger.

Lowell said, "All right. If that's how it is, I'll speak to Hadfield. Get him for me." And when the connection was made he said, "Mr. Hadfield, you asked certain questions a few minutes ago which both Neil and myself believe should be answered directly and fully. I regret very much, however, that such answers are impossible at the present time. The most serious issues are involved, bearing upon our basic relationship to InterCos, our loyalty to its principles, and so on; and I can only ask you to rely on our integrity and not press us for an immediate statement."

Hadfield said, "It's as serious as that, Mr. Secretary?"

"It's as serious as that."

"If the circumstances worsen, will the American Delegation walk out?"

"What put that idea into your head?"

"Just a hunch. I assume you're having differences of opinion with Dr. Werner."

"We can't walk out, Mr. Hadfield. We're all in this together."

"And you feel that no information should be given to the public at present?"

"It's not a matter of what I feel. The American Delegation is still absolutely bound by the Covenant of Inter-Cos. We can't act without authorization from the Council of Ministers or the Supreme Commander. We can't individually divulge classified information. If Balatov did so to the Russian people, or Hsuen to the Chinese people, we would shout bloody murder, and so would you.—But let me say this: I'm informed that the Supreme Commander is contemplating another global broadcast at nine o'clock. This is not yet official. If he does *not* *make* this broadcast, or if he makes a broadcast which does *not* answer your questions, I shall be glad to talk to you again. In the meantime, I should be grateful if you would honor my confidence and not publish any of this conversation."

"I understand," Hadfield said. "Thank you, sir."

Hart called a few minutes later. "I have a bulletin from the Supreme Commander. He will broadcast at nine o'clock."

"Thanks for letting me know, Hart."

"Working very hard, Neil? How about taking a break, eh? Meet me in the lounge——"

"Sorry, Hart. Impossible."

"Dinner, then. Eh?"

"I'm having a sandwich sent up. Sorry."

"All right, Neil. Maybe later."

A weariness seemed to have settled over the entire organization of InterCos. Except for the continuing flood of incoming calls, there was little to do. The Committee of Five showed no signs of life: all five men might have perished in that locked room ninety feet below ground. The newly appointed military advisors wandered from room to room in a desultory fashion, waiting hopefully for an opportunity to advise somebody about something; but no opportunity came. Hooper, the new deputy, settled down to a methodical reorganization of the Delegation's filing system and almost drove Neil out of his mind by trotting in every few minutes with armfuls of files and asking, "Is this important, Harrison? Should we keep this? Harrison, I see that Document 85MX is duplicated by Document 109MB—must we keep both?" Neil eventually snapped at him, "If you don't have anything better to do, for heaven's sake, take over my desk for half an hour," and stamped out to see Mark.

Mark was resting. Ismay and Luden were sitting gloomily in Room 6509, and Ismay said curtly as soon as Neil entered, "You can't see him."

"What's wrong?"

"Nothing. He's asleep. I gave him a shot after you left this afternoon. It'll probably carry him through the night."

"How is he?"

"Bad."

Luden said, in an attempt to sound encouraging, "He'll feel a lot better after a good sleep."

"That's true," Ismay said. He stood up. "Care to get a breath of fresh air, Neil?"

Neil nodded.

Ismay turned to Luden. "Is that all right? Or would you prefer to go now?"

"I can wait," Luden said. "I don't like the smell of that air out there tonight."

Ismay said, "Come on, Neil."

They went out into the corridor, and as they passed Room 6509 Neil heard the sound of a recording being played. He halted and listened, and then said to Ismay,

"Would you mind if I look in on Jordan Woolley for one minute?"

"Go ahead."

Neil walked into the room. Jordan, sleepy-eyed, was leaning against a wall listening to the noise coming from a tape machine. He said weakly, "Hi, Neil."

"Hi.—What's this?"

"The latest from the Ampiti."

Neil's lips tightened.

"Fun, eh?" Jordan said. His sleepy eyes became sad. "It's been going on like this for the past two hours."

The noise was simply a continuous ululation, maintained—it seemed—by hundreds of voices.

"I thought it was a dirge," Jordan said, smiling nervously. "You know: a funeral chant. But how can they keep it up all this time?"

"Not a word of sense?" Neil asked.

"No," Jordan answered. "Not even *kobley-kobley.*" He laughed. "I keep thinking of the good old days when they used to sound positively intellectual. Remember? *Ne marta parta, hu-hu, ne kommen, hu-hu, paykay paylay hu-hu. . . .* This stuff is just moronic. It's getting on my nerves."

La-la-la-la, the tape machine wailed. *La-la-la-la, la-a la-a, la-la-la-la, la-a, la-a, la-la-la-la, la-a, la-a, la-la-la-la- . . .* The chorus went on and on, with the same rising and falling note: *La-la-la-la, la-a, la-a, la-la-la-la, la-a, la-a,* until Jordan switched it off.

"Like an institution full of insane children," Jordan said.

Even with the machine silent, the sound continued to ring in Neil's ears. *La-la-la-la, la-a, la-a, . . . La-la-la-la, la-a, la-a . . .*

"I'm not a semanticist," Jordan said. He seemed anxious to talk, to open the floodgates. "But up to yesterday I was beginning to think I understood what the Ampiti were saying. I was feeling it in my bones, somehow. Maybe it was the result of living with the noise day after day. I wouldn't call myself an expert, like Mark or Libby.

But all the same, I felt it. It hit me somewhere in the solar plexus. . . . You know?"

He rubbed the back of his neck nervously. "It was like somebody shouting to you in Hindustani or Arabic, *Don't come down this road, it's loaded with dynamite.* You . . . sort of . . . get the gist of it. The sense. As you do when you're listening to music. It . . . sort of . . . stirs you. You feel sure you understand what the composer meant." He stopped, and made an oddly helpless gesture with his hands.

"Yes," Neil said. "I think I know what you mean!"

"I understand there were quite a few semanticists who agreed with Mark and Libby," Jordan went on. "Even some here, at InterCos. Dr. Werner didn't approve, though. They were transferred to other duties." His eyes dimmed. "Now we're getting this. Dancing dervishes. Mad, completely mad. I'd give a month's pay if they'd go back to *kobley-kobley.*"

Neil said, "Let me know if the noises change."

"Sure," Jordan said. "Sure." He was staring blankly at the wall.

Neil said, "I'll see you later," and rejoined Ismay.

They went down in the elevator and walked in silence through the imposing Arabian glass corridor and then out into the Grand Plaza. It was the first time Neil had left the building all day.

The fountains were playing, the floodlights were on as usual, the flags were fluttering in the night breeze. But there was a strange sickly smell in the air, and Neil sniffed, wrinkled his nose, and asked, "What's this stench?"

"The green stuff on the Hudson."

"You mean, you can smell it at this distance?"

"That's right."

Neil swore.

"Queer stuff," Ismay said calmly. "It burns anything it touches. It grows, almost the way yeast grows. And it's metallic—it deflects a compass needle. Are you acquainted with any substance that has all those physical qualities?"

"No."

"Neither am I. Mark calculated this morning, when he first heard about it, that in a week it will have covered most of Manhattan."

"That's swell," Neil said heavily.

Ismay turned to look at the Palace of InterCos. He said, "It's a beautiful building. Very strongly constructed. I guess we'll be safe enough up on the sixty-fifth floor. Unless, of course, this stuff eats through walls. Or can climb——"

They walked on a little way, and Ismay added, "My wife and children are in Washington. I called this evening and told Lena to take the kids over to my mother in Maryland. They've found some of this green stuff in the Potomac, you know."

"Yes," Neil said. "I saw a bulletin about that."

The Grand Plaza was surprisingly crowded. Neil looked at the faces of the people he passed, and they all seemed a little bewildered but at the same time hopeful, as if they were confident that within this splendid glass structure there was the power, the strength, the wisdom to drive away all the doubts that had begun to trouble them. They had heard strange rumors; they had come here to have those rumors answered. They had come here to be assured that the visitors hovering in the night sky, the curious weed in the Hudson, were not malevolent, did not menace their well-being; and merely staring up at the Palace of InterCos appeared to give them comfort. *Our jewel box, holding man's wildest and most exciting dreams——*

Here was the replica of the Cologne rocket, the first rocket to carry men more than two hundred and fifty miles above the surface of the earth. Its crew had died, or course; but not in vain. For a noble dream. And here was a replica of the Bartholomew rocket, one of the most famous of all—the rocket that served as the foundation stone of Platform Alpha. And here was a replica of R1001, the first to reach Moon from Alpha; and here was Rocket Werner, named in honor of the President of InterCos (now its Supreme Commander) which had blazed the way to New Panama.

All floodlit. All with needle-noses pointing skyward, straining for the blast-off. All beautiful and heavy with power; but in reality empty. Only replicas.

And here was the great Ad Astra, built on a pediment of Martian mineral-bearing rock which the first convoys had brought from New Panama on their return flights, at Dr. Werner's order. The group of statuary was conventional, perhaps, two tall figures—a girl and a young man—reaching up to the stars; but the sculptors had been whipped into a creative fury by Dr. Werner's eloquence, and these two enormous, long-legged, naked creatures *reached,* as if they were trying to claw the stars out of the heavens; every muscle, every fiber, every atom of the shining bronze bodies seemed to flow upward with a wild yearning to reach, to capture, to hold and possess the blackness overhead and the prizes burning in that darkness.

At the foot of the group was another replica; a model of the Beta Complex as it would appear on completion.

"Sometimes I wonder," Ismay said.

Neil, absorbed in his own thoughts, said, "What, Bernie?"

"Never mind," Ismay said; but a moment later he said, "I'll tell you the truth. I was never really impressed by all that talk Dr. Werner put out—you know, about turning Mars into a garden, and so on and so forth. I always wondered, what about turning Earth into a garden first?—Reactionary, I suppose. Eh?"

"Very reactionary."

"Do you have great ambitions to be the instrument of a purpose?" Ismay asked.

"Not any more."

Ismay laughed sardonically. "Ah. You're a reactionary, too." He looked up at the Ad Astra, the two star-reaching figures. "If this green stuff grows like yeast there's no reason why it should stop anywhere, is there? I mean, it can spread across everything. The stuff in the Hudson will spread across New Jersey until it meets the stuff

142

from the Potomac that has spread across Maryland——"

"Feeling morbid?" Neil asked.

"No. I'm in love with my wife," Ismay said. "And my kids are a pain in the neck, like Mark's kids, but I love them too, for some reason." He was still looking up at the Ad Astra. "I wish somebody would take that pair of monkeys down. They'd be much happier sitting on a park bench holding hands." He sighed. "I forgot. We don't believe in love any more. It's an archaic word, found only in pre-InterCos literature.—Let's go back. This smell is beginning to pinch my nostrils."

A survey made during the Supreme Commander's broadcast showed that approximately 1.973 per cent of the global tele audience was receiving the speech—an appreciable increase over the previous night's figure, when only 1.028 per cent took the trouble to listen. The experts were able to deduce two important facts from these simple statistics. Firstly, more people were taking an interest in current affairs (in the experts' words) which was a healthy sign. Secondly, there were still far too many people who apparently preferred to play three-dimensional checkers or other indoor games and did not give a fig for current affairs. More than 98 per cent. This, the head of Dr. Werner's survey organization said angrily, would have to be corrected. Far too many people were pursuing their own selfish ends and did not realize the vital part that InterCos contributed to their lives.

The Supreme Commander, in a white uniform for this occasion, seemed to be tired; but he still spoke with fire. His address was mostly introduction: InterCos, the dream, the fulfillment, the peace-loving eagerness to bring new life, new hope, to the barren places in our solar system, the great plans for vast superbly engineered waterways that would make Mars a paradise, the great plans for Platform Beta which was to serve as an island in space for universal cultural exchange and perhaps for unimagined universal commerce. "Never once," he said, "have we swerved from our greatest, our most precious ideal; that all we accomplish must be ac-

complished in peace. By peaceful means. Not by the
sword; but by patience, kindness, understanding and
love. Love. This word that has almost died out of our
vocabulary, but has remained embedded in our hearts
like an untarnishable diamond."

(*What does he mean,* Neil thought angrily. *Too many
people are using this word nowadays. Love.* And he
wondered whether Libby was watching and listening to
Dr. Werner, and how she was reacting to this long, emotional speech which had been made—with variations—
so often before.)

But the Supreme Commander was soon brief and to
the point. He said (and he seemed to grow taller as he
spoke): "I now bring you some tragic facts. Last night
I told you that we had become aware of certain flying
objects which had entered our space zone. I described
them as visitors, and I hoped they came to us as friends.
This has proven to be erroneous. In the last twenty-four
hours there have been several hostile attacks on our
cities which have been definitely traced to these visitors.
Furthermore, some noxious chemical has been planted in
many of our waterways, which our scientists are now engaged in neutralizing. There has been loss of life. There
has been damage to property. But, let me stress this
point, these attacks are trivial compared to the frightful
retribution that we can hurl at an enemy when we begin
in earnest to defend ourselves.

"This defense is now being prepared by my Cabinet.
If we continue to be subjected to unprovoked attack we
shall move to protect ourselves with pitiless strength. Yet,
I beg of you, do not be impatient. I have one hope:
that peace can be maintained, that these tragic events
have resulted from misunderstanding. I shall make yet
another attempt to establish contact with the fleets that
are trespassing on our space zones. I shall do all in my
power to negotiate an honorable settlement. In the meantime, our defense plans will go ahead. We have appointed a Director of Public Safety who, in the event
of further hostilities, will be responsible for steps to
safeguard you and your families. He will speak to you

144

in a few minutes. Trust him. He will be your friend and guide."

The Supreme Commander's speech must have made a deep impression on his global audience. Soon after he concluded, the survey department noted that 2.537 per cent of all telesets were now tuned to the InterCos channel, and this figure was gradually rising. There seemed to be a growing interest in current affairs, the head of the survey department said with satisfaction; and he was delighted to see that his public-reaction meters showed an upward swing to 3.806 per cent when the new Director of Public Safety came before the InterCos tele cameras.

He was an imposing man, big and patriarchal, with a long curling white beard and a deep, gentle voice. Neil, watching him in the company of SecState Lowell, General Kirkland, and Admiral Gould, had the impression that he might at any moment address his audience as "my children." He was an Indian, chosen from Dhevu's Delegation. Formerly he had been Professor of Moral Philosophy at the University of Bombay.

He said, "Dear peoples of the world: in these bewildering times we must have faith; we must have confidence; above all we must not panic." He repeated this advice and enlarged on it for a quarter of an hour. Then he said, "Now, my dear people, I want to tell you this. If you hear a loud noise in the sky which might be a bomb or a missile coming toward you, please lie down under a bed or a table, and shield your head with your arms. Remember: lie down, under a bed or a table——"

Kirkland burst into raucous laughter.

Gould said in his harsh, leathery voice, "Who is this old man, Mr. Secretary? What does he know about public safety?"

Lowell said, "Probably nothing. However, he can go to town on the Bhagavad-Gita."

Gould said, "Eh?"

Lowell explained, "What I meant to say was, it's a political appointment."

Kirkland's laughter stopped abruptly. "Look here, Mr. Secretary, this isn't a time for political appointments. That's a key job. The man who holds it ought to know what he's doing."

Lowell said, "Neil, let's have your opinion. Why did Werner make this appointment?"

Neil said bitterly, "I guess it's the old, old story. I guess the Committee of Five is split, and Werner's trying to swing Dhevu over by appointing an Indian to this vitally important spot."

"That's about how I would size it up, too," Lowell said. He looked at Kirkland, then at Gould. He said to Neil, "Would you mind switching the teleset off?"

Neil did so.

"I've been sitting in this office all evening," Lowell said, "trying to figure out what's happening down below with the Committee of Five; and I've come to certain conclusions now, which this last broadcast tends to confirm. Anybody care to listen to an old man's ideas?"

Gould said, "Go ahead please, Mr. Secretary. I'm just an infant toddling through the wilderness."

"Consider me in the same category," Kirkland said.

"All right," Lowell said. "Let's try to imagine how Werner is thinking at the present time. He's a tough character, you know. He'll fight to the bitter end for the thing he believes in. He won't knuckle under to the Ampiti unless he's literally forced to."

Lowell paused to suck at his cold pipe, then lit it. "So far, Werner's been fairly cautious. He's only taken relatively small-scale action against the Ampiti—reactivating the workshops, sending up three or four battle wagons. True, he's lost a couple of battle wagons, but that may have been due to other causes, inexperienced flight personnel, and so on. But what has he learned about the opposing forces? Primarily the thing that you pointed out, Kirkland: their striking power seems to be almost negligible. Their missiles, compared to our f-type weapons, are picayune. You had an estimate this after-

146

noon, didn't you?" He addressed the question at Kirkland.

"Yes, sir. They're using missiles roughly equivalent to a twentieth-century 250-pound high-explosive bomb. That's nonatomic, of course. And they're dropping them only in ones or twos. The most primitive aircraft did better than that even in World War I."

"Precisely," Lowell said. "And as for the green stuff, Werner must feel, like nearly everybody else, that our scientists can deal with that in short order. Right. These, I believe, are the arguments Werner is using with the Committee of Five. He is pointing out that the Ampiti are militarily weak. Despite the shock of finding them in our space zones, we have no real reason to fear them. If we capitulate to them now, Man's empire in space will be lost for all time. Let us, by all means, continue with our offers to negotiate, but let us be careful to surrender nothing; and if the Ampiti are obstinate, let us muster all our strength and wipe them from the skies to show them, once and for all, who is boss. I figure that Crandall and Vernon strongly oppose this policy; Balatov and Hsuen are for it; and Dhevu is sitting on the fence. That is why all Werner's broadcasts have effectively said nothing; and that is why the Indian gentleman with the long, white beard has been appointed Director of Public Safety."

He asked, after a moment, "Anybody disagree with that line of reasoning?"

Gould rubbed his hands together briskly. "It makes sense to me. Politics. Always a tricky business. However, I'll say this: I don't like this fellow Werner and I don't care for his methods, but I can't help being impressed by his attitude. I like a man who's ready to fight for something he believes in. What's wrong with that?"

"Nothing," Lowell answered, "if it's a barroom brawl. But in this case I'm inclined to agree with Mark Harrison, whose opinion is that if we fight we'll be annihilated."

"Who do you mean by *we*?" Gould said in a growl.

"You and me," Lowell said with a faint smile. "Not to mention the rest of the human race."

Soon after midnight three missiles fell in Brooklyn. A special watchdog service initiated by InterCos reported that missiles had fallen in threes almost simultaneously in some hundred and five cities, involving practically all world capitals. The damage was most severe in Buenos Aires where a hotel was hit, the missile exploding on the glass-enclosed roof garden where a dance was in progress.

Jerre Hadfield called Neil again immediately after these explosions, and SecState Lowell agreed to talk with him. Hadfield said, "Mr. Secretary, I wasn't impressed by Dr Werner's broadcast, but I thought I wouldn't trouble you until morning. Now there's been a new attack—three bombs on Brooklyn: eleven people killed and twenty-five injured. Three on Chicago, St. Louis, San Francisco, London, and Paris, and more reports coming in from our field men. I think you ought to make an immediate statement."

"I still can't make a statement, Mr. Hadfield. I'm still bound by the rules of InterCos. There hasn't been a meeting of the Council of Ministers at which I could raise the issue."

"Are we in a war with the Ampiti?"

"As far as I know, the Supreme Commander is not ready to call it war. He's still trying to negotiate."

"Is the American Delegation giving Dr Werner its wholehearted support?"

"The American Delegation reserves the right to express opposition to any InterCos policy, but it is obliged to accept the decision of the majority in the Council of Ministers. That is expressly laid down in the Covenant, Mr. Hadfield."

"Do you feel Dr. Werner's policies have led to the present situation?"

"It would be highly improper for me to criticize Dr. Werner publicly, whatever I think of his leadership."

"May I quote that?"

"No, sir, I'm afraid you may not."

148

"Speaking as an American, not as an editor, purely as an American citizen, have we or have we not surrendered our sovereignty, Mr. Secretary?"

"Mr. Hadfield: in the world today, as you know, we cannot act as individual nations. We are a part of Inter-Cos and we must stay a part of InterCos. We may criticize it, we may be alarmed by some of its policies, but we would be lunatics if we attempted to destroy it. As things stand, our nation has a full voice in the Council of Ministers and a representative in the defense cabinet. We also have allies, who concur with us on practically all points, so we are not alone. We cannot ask for any more than that." Lowell paused, and then went on: "You may quote that statement, if you like. I don't think anybody can take exception to it, here or outside."

"If I may say so, sir, it doesn't give the man in the street very clear guidance."

"You think not?"

"No, sir. I'm being blunt, and it's my job to be blunt. We're being bombed, people are being killed, and we have a right to know whether our leadership is sound or not."

Lowell glanced round at Neil, as if for encouragement, and then said, "All right. Here are one or two ideas that you might like to kick around editorially. You might even like to arrange for fairly wide distribution . . . with the proviso that you don't attribute them to me, or anybody who works for me."

"Go ahead, sir," Hadfield said urgently.

"You could start like this," Lowell said: "Many informed observers believe that InterCos, under its Supreme Commander Dr. Werner, is about to lead our planet to its doom. Ever since the Voices of the Ampiti were heard nearly a year ago, Dr. Werner has refused to heed any warnings that would impede his ambitions of a superempire extending to the furthest galaxies in space." Lowell continued steadily for ten minutes. He ended: "Now we are being bombarded by those beings whom Dr. Werner has so consistently defied. A new kind of chemical warfare has begun, which threatens our ports and all water-borne transportation. Dr. Werner, in this emergency, continues to play politics by appointing as Director of Public Safety a man who may have an admirable record as a scholar but who obviously has no grasp of the practical realities of his task. We call for an end to all this. It is probably too late; but possibly honest men can still save us. Werner must go. The human race can no longer tolerate or afford his leadership."

Lowell stopped, meditatively.

Hadfield waited, and then asked, "Any more, sir?"

"That's enough for the time being," Lowell said. He smiled at Hadfield's attentive image on the tele screen. "Just a few random thoughts, which you might be able to develop."

"Yes, Mr. Secretary. We'll develop them." Hadfield's voice was grim.

"Remember," Lowell said, "I didn't make this statement. I should be thrown out of InterCos if anybody discovered that I had anything to do with it."

"I understand," Hadfield said. "I'll get to work right away."

When the screen darkened Lowell turned to Neil. He sounded defiant. He said, "I've been wanting to make that speech for a long time. Now, I'm afraid it's too late."

Neil said, "Let's hope not." A polite remark, a diplomatic remark, but not really convincing. He was thinking of Libby.

At six o'clock the next morning four missiles hit the Greenwich Village area in New York. Simultaneously, the InterCos watchdog service reported, 136 cities throughout the world had been attacked in the same way.

The global percentage of telesets tuned to the InterCos channel was now 11.673; once again, a record for this hour of the day.

The Turkish Minister called SecState Lowell to inform him that according to messages received from Istanbul, missiles had fallen in the vicinity of the InterCos workshops at Sahara and Lake Baikal. No definite estimate was yet available of the damage that had been inflicted.

Sir Alton Berkeley called SecState Lowell to inform him that a hospital in the East End of London had been hit. "Seventy-eight people killed," Berkeley said, in a rage that he could scarcely control. "Mostly women patients and nurses."

SecState Lowell expressed shock and sympathy.

"It was one of these new hospital buildings," Berkeley said. "All glass. The glass did most of the damage." Then he said, "We'll have to hit back. We can't go on like this."

"How can we hit back?" SecState Lowell asked.

Berkeley said, "Blast them out of the sky."

Washington reported that four missiles had landed in the vicinity of the Octagon. General Kirkland commented acidly, "Best thing that's happened there in forty years."

Locke called SecState Lowell to inform him that Wellington had been hit. His government was deeply concerned.

"We're all concerned," SecState Lowell said.

At eight o'clock the Director of Public Safety broadcast to approximately 13.496 per cent of all global telesets. He suggested putting adhesive tape or wire mesh over windows, and turning mirrors so that they faced walls. He said, "My dear people, keep your baths filled with water, and if you hear a loud noise which might be a bomb or a missile coming toward you, hurry to shelter. Lie down under a bed or a table, with hands protecting the back of the head. Please do not panic."

The police in New York reported heavy traffic over the George Washington Bridge. The Lincoln and Eisenhower Tunnels were being closed owing to the presence of noxious fumes believed to come from the green fungus on the Hudson.

The switchboard at InterCos were closed to incoming calls from the public inquiring about InterCos policy.

SecState Lowell called the acting President of Inter-Cos, requesting an emergency session of the Council of Ministers. The acting President, very gratefully, said that he himself had intended to call such a meeting but had been advised by the Director of Public Safety that the Council Chamber was hazardous because it was almost totally enclosed by glass. "We are getting reports of so many casualties from glass," the acting President explained.

"There's glass everywhere in this building," SecState Lowell said. "Does that mean the Council of Ministers ceases to function from now on?"

The acting President said that there was a possibility that the InterCos Concert Hall, on the fourteenth floor, might be taken over for Council meetings. The Concert Hall was relatively safe because the walls were lined with acoustic materials——

"Mr. President," SecState Lowell said, "I hesitate to apply the whip, but I suggest you do something now. This minute."

The acting President called back almost at once to say that the Council would convene in the Concert Hall at ten o'clock.

At a quarter to nine Neil met Jordan Woolley in the corridor. Neil asked, "How's Mark?"

"He's not up yet," Jordan said. "I haven't seen him. Bernie is making him rest as much as possible."

"Does he know about these explosions?"

"I doubt it. He's full of dope."

"Anything new from the Voices?"

"No," Jordan said. "They're just ululating like mad."

Bulletins began to pour into the Delegation office about the green metallic fungus. It was spreading rapidly on the Hudson and the Potomac. It was reported also in the St. Lawrence River, the Mississippi, the Snake River, and other North American waterways. It had also appeared (SecState Lowell noted with interest) in the Ganges; and a remarkable phenomenon reported from this area was that the Indian police were having difficulty preventing sections of the public from committing mass suicide by immersing themselves in the substance. It had not yet been isolated by any scientists owing to the difficulty of obtaining samples.

At nine-thirty five missiles hit the west side of New York, doing a great deal of damage. Simultaneous bombings occurred in 139 cities. The watchdog service amended this to 141 cities, later to 143.

Neil remembered, *I promised to get to Libby today. How can I leave InterCos, with all this happening? But I have to see her today. Somehow I must see her today.*

The Council of Ministers met at ten o'clock, listened nervously to speeches from SecState Lowell, the Polish Minister, the Spanish and Portuguese Ministers (apologizing for their behavior yesterday), and a poetic address by Madame Ai-Wen-Tai. The acting President read a bulletin from the Committee of Five, stating that after prolonged deliberation three squadrons of interceptors armed with f-type weapons had been ordered to carry out continuous patrols between Earth and Platform Alpha. These squadrons were under the strictest instructions not to engage in combat with any unidentified space craft, except in the following clearly defined circumstances: (a) if such craft were observed attacking Earth, and (b) in self-defense.

This bulletin was followed by a message from the Supreme Commander, in which he announced that he would address the Council of Ministers at eleven o'clock over the Red circuit. After reading this, the acting President promptly adjourned the meeting.

Sir Alton Berkeley joined SecState Lowell to listen to the Supreme Commander; so did McAllister, Waterson, and Locke. As they waited for the address to begin they sat very quietly. Neil remembered how they had sat here three nights ago, arguing, planning, trying to forge a joint policy which would give them control of this situation. They had failed, of course. Werner was too strongly entrenched. But if they had succeeded, would the situation now be different? Neil did not know. The past three days, after all, were only a tiny fragment of human history. What had Mark called it—chicanery. The chicanery had been going on too long, for hundreds of thousands of years. It was improbable that it could be eradicated from the human system in the course of sixty or seventy hours.

The Supreme Commander began to speak punctually at eleven. He said very little at great length. The only new facts he had to give the Ministers were that the number of interceptor squadrons had been increased from three to ten, and another three large defense craft had been added to those already in action. He still hoped for successful negotiations, but there had been no response from the Ampiti. He promised a further report to the Ministers in the early part of the afternoon.

When he finished, Locke said, "Isn't all this a waste of time? A complete waste of time? What good are we doing sitting here?" It was an impulsive outburst, and he immediately apologized for it.

McAllister said, "I wish we'd hear from Crandall or Vernon. At least, we'd know what's going on."

"They're fighting the good fight," Berkeley said with a whimsical smile. "We can be sure of that, even if we never set eyes on them again."

Waterson stood up and said angrily, "The great advantage of talking over the Red circuit is that nobody can answer back. I'd like to ask our revered Supreme Commander a few questions, but I might just as well sit in a corner and talk to myself. I'm just as useful as a sick dog."

Berkeley said quietly, "I've been thinking something of the same kind. In fact, I've been thinking of handing everything over to Stevens and taking the first plane back to London."

"No," Lowell said. "No. Hang on. I know how you

154

feel. But our job is here. We'll be needed. Hang on."

The sixth salvo fell at one o'clock. In New York, the six missiles fell in a ragged circle around Grand Central Station, fortunately missing the big helicopter terminal. One, however, fell some distance away, on a dress designer's studio in Madison Avenue, blowing out the top floor where nine young models were being fitted with clothes for a fashion show that afternoon. In London, another hospital was hit, without very serious casualties this time. In Berlin, it was at first reported that one of the missiles had failed to explode and had been dug up intact; but this was later denied. The number of cities under bombardment was now stabilized by the InterCos watchdog service at 143; and the most serious cause of casualties was reported to be flying glass. The Director of Public Safety spoke about the dangers of glass and urged the dear peoples of the world to keep the curtains drawn over their windows. He begged everybody to remain calm.

Extremely heavy traffic was reported across the George Washington Bridge, and also the Triborough Bridge. Temporary failure of air control on the East Side aerial highway caused a pile up involving several passenger helicopters; and as a result the lanes were being temporarily closed. In Madrid, a mob shouting—for obscure reasons—"Down with Portugal" was dispersed by the Civil Guard. On the banks of the Ganges, seventeen religious devotees were successful in eluding the police and immersing themselves in the green metallic fungus. Their bodies had not been recovered.

9

THE PATTERN was now clear. Everybody in InterCos now knew that there would be seven missiles in the next salvo, approximately at three o'clock, and that about two hours later there would be another salvo, the eighth, consisting of eight missiles, and that this process would go on until it was stopped.

Until it was stopped, in some manner yet unclear. The Lords of InterCos met in their large, splendid offices and discussed among themselves, bloc by bloc, how to stop the missiles from falling, but they found it exceedingly difficult to arrive at any practical conclusion. They could only agree that in the final analysis the responsibility for stopping the bombardment rested with the Committee of Five and with the Supreme Commander.

The Supreme Commander acted quickly, and with impressive decision. At one-thirty, soon after the sixth salvo had fallen, he removed the dewy-eyed, white-bearded Indian from the post of Director of Public Safety and appointed in his place a Norwegian. The new Director, in a global address, advised the citizens of the world to keep their windows curtained, their bath filled with water; also, to assemble first-aid kits; also, to keep tuned for further broadcasts which would demonstrate how to apply a tourniquet to a severe wound; also, to keep children indoors; also, to volunteer for ambulance duties, since the hospitals in most cities were understaffed.

Lowell said, "That's a hopeful sign. Dhevu is probably being obstinate. Werner must be having trouble, if he has to find a scapegoat so soon."

Neil was alone with him in Crandall's office. He said, "Mr. Secretary, are you still hoping everything can be solved by a political change, a change in leadership?"

"I can't see anything else," Lowell replied. "If we can throw Werner out . . . put Vernon in. . . ." His voice trailed away.

"And then what?"

"Frankly, I haven't thought it through, Neil."

"We offer the Ampiti a peaceful settlement?"

"We can't offer anything else."

"In what language?" Neil asked. "How do we reach them? How do we tell them we want peace?"

"I was hoping Mark could advise us about that."

"He's still sleeping. I was in there a few minutes ago. Ismay told me that apparently all the activity of the past few days has weakened him so much that the dope he took yesterday has knocked him out."

Lowell looked up in alarm. "Is it serious?"

"No. He needs all the rest he can get. This sleep ought to do him good."

Lowell tapped nervously against the edge of the table. "You're right about this language problem, this communication problem. I've been having nightmares over it. Sure: even if Vernon takes over, how do we talk to the Ampiti? In Chinese, or Dutch, or Hindustani? I've been hoping Mark could advise us about that. Now we don't have Mark—we can't be sure of having him. Who else is there?" He bit his lip. "What about Jordan Woolley?"

"Jordan is an astro-physicist. Language isn't his line."

"What about that girl who was here the other afternoon? Dr. Hewes. Wasn't she a semanticist?"

"Yes, sir."

"We should have thought of this before," Lowell said. "Get her in here. See if *she* has any ideas."

"Very well." Neil turned to leave.

"Wait a minute. Didn't Mark say something about you being fond of her?"

157

"Yes."

"You're hoping to marry her—didn't Mark say that?"

Neil replied quietly, "We were planning to get married next week."

Lowell looked away. "Congratulations."

"Thank you."

"I only met her for a moment, but I liked her very much." He smiled, half-humorously, half in pity. "I hope you're going to ask me to the ceremony. Both Crandall and myself. You must, you know."

"Of course, sir."

"Good," Lowell said. He still could not look at the younger man. He said, "In the meantime, will you ask her to be kind enough to come to InterCos, so that we may have the benefit of her experience on these semantic questions? We should appreciate it very much."

Neil said, "Yes," and left the room.

There was no reply from the apartment. He called the house in Central Park and spoke to Evelyn. Libby had not been there.

Evelyn said, "If she calls I'll ask her to get in touch with you immediately."

"Thanks, Evie."

"She's a sweet girl and we all love her dearly.—Neil. Tell me, please. How's my husband?"

"He's fine."

"Honest?"

"Honest. He's having a whale of a time, telling everybody in sight what nincompoops they are."

"That sounds like my man. Will you let me know if he needs me, at any time?"

"Of course. And if I get a chance I'll drop by."

She said, "Don't worry about me, Neil. I have the three Dobermans in the house, and I'm not lonesome. Your job is to take care of Libby Hewes."

He laughed. "Yes. When and if I find her."

He switched off and went to Room 6509. Luden was alone. The door leading to 6508 was ajar, and Luden nodded toward it and said, "Bernie is in there with Mark."

"Is he awake yet?"

"No."

Neil said, "Look, Griff, you can tell me the truth. He has never slept like this before. What's happening to him?"

Luden answered uncomfortably, "We aren't sure. He seems to be in a coma. But we can't discern any serious deterioration in his physical condition. Just a slight drop in temperature. Of course, he's still under considerable mental strain——"

"What do you mean?"

"He's talking all the time. A sort of delirium."

"Sort of," Neil repeated. "What do you mean, a *sort* of delirium?"

"Go in, if you like," Luden said. "Listen for yourself."

Mark was half sitting, half lying in the big wheel chair, swathed in blankets. His eyes were closed, his mouth open, and he was breathing with difficulty. Ismay, looking haggard, turned angrily when Neil entered and then relaxed. Jordan Woolley was sitting at Mark's side, operating a tape recorder.

Neil said in a low voice, "How is he, Bernie?"

"He's alive. That's all we know. You don't have to whisper. He can't hear a thing we say, apparently."

"Should we call Evelyn?"

"No," Ismay said. "He'll come out of this sometime in the next few hours."

Mark began to mumble. The words sounded like, S—ben—arn . . . s—ben—arn . . . fi—ben—arn . . .

Ismay turned to Neil. "He repeats that over and over. Any idea what it means?"

"What else does he keep repeating?"

"Jordan has it on tape."

"I can make a guess at *ben—arn*," Neil said. "Benedict Arnold."

Ismay stared at him.

"*Find Benedict Arnold,*" Neil said. There was no time

now to explain. He turned to Jordan. "I'd like to hear the tape."

"Sure," Jordan said. He stood up and breathed in deeply. He was haggard, too. "Come next door."

He played three tapes; but there was nothing significant on them, only the mumbled repetition of *s—ben—arn, fi—ben—arn*, the name *Ampiti* repeated frequently, and painful cries of *No, no, mustn't, mustn't* and then the name *Evelyn, Evelyn*, surprisingly clear after the choked articulation of the other. But as the fourth tape began to run Jordan said, "This is the best of them. Some of it seems to make sense in a way. I was going to bring it in to you." He added. "It's a pity Libby isn't with us. She'd probably elucidate it without any trouble."

"I'm hoping to bring her here."

"You are?" Jordan said, and sighed. "That's good. Even though it's rather late."

There was a babble of words from the recording machine. "Green—green—yes, yes—la, la, la, la—green, yes, green, yes. . . ."

Jordan said, "This is the section. Listen."

"Green, green," Mark chattered. "Green, green—burn, burn—green burn, green, burn, metal, why?—Negative, positive, neg, pos, metal, green, see?—Circuit, see? Keep circuit, green, burn, green grow, grass grow—"

"Wait a minute!" Jordan cried. "Wait a minute! I think I know—"

"Be quiet," Neil said. "Let me hear this."

"Fight, circuit, fight, circuit, press switch, fight, circuit, green-green, green-circuit, la-la-la-la, circuit green, green grows, keep circuit, green grows, metal, metal—"

It had the singsong rhythm of the latest Ampiti broadcasts, the same insistence, without beginning or end. After several minutes Neil said, "Switch it off, Jordan. I can't take it." He sat down, feeling weak.

Jordan switched off the noise.

"Well?" Neil said. "What does it mean?"

"I'm a fool," Jordan said. "I should have spotted it at once. I must be asleep." He was smiling, the detached inward smile of a scientist. "This green stuff. It's metallic. Why? Because it's part of an electrical circuit. That's what Mark is trying to say. Don't you understand?"

"No. Is that important?"

Jordan shrugged his shoulders. "Only academically, I suppose. Mark's thought seems to be that as long as the Ampiti keep the circuit in operation the green stuff will continue to grow. *Press switch, green grows. Fight, circuit, fight, circuit.*—That is, it'll grow while the fighting continues."

Neil shivered unexpectedly. "You think that's possible?"

Jordan rubbed his forehead. "Why not?"

"And they can keep that switch on until this stuff covers everything?"

"Or——" Jordan began, and stopped. In the next room Mark had begun to shout violently.

Neil swung round and hurried in.

Luden and Ismay were struggling to hold the huge body down. Mark's eyes were still closed, but he was fighting and shouting as if a demon had taken possession of him. "Evelyn! Evelyn! Save Evelyn! The boys, Evelyn! Ben Arnold, save Evelyn and the boys! Ben Arnold, save Evelyn, Evelyn, Evelyn——"

Ismay snarled at Neil, "Get out of here. Get out!"

"Let me help——"

"We can manage," Luden panted. "Leave him to us."

Outside in the corridor he bumped blindly against a man and said in vague apology, "I beg your pardon," and, looking up, saw that the man was Hart von Horstmann. The vagueness, the shock of Mark's madness, left him, and he said angrily, "What are you doing up here?"

"Hi, Neil."

"I asked you: what are you doing up here, Hart?"

Hart laughed. "*Flagrante delicto.* . . . As a matter of fact, old chap, I was hoping that I could meet your brother for a minute. I admire him very much, you remember——"

Neil took his arm and led him away. "I've told you.

He's sick. He can't see anybody. I've told you that several times already."

Hart gently released Neil's grip. He was unexpectedly strong; and he looked very golden at this moment, very handsome, young, untroubled. Neil's anger, and the larger anger of the unknown forces in the skies over-head, seemed to have no effect on his gaiety. He said, smiling brightly, "You guard your brother so well. I as-sure you, I only wished to say a few words to him——"

Neil said, "Go and tell Werner he's sick. And don't try to get in to see him again. There are three men in there with him, and they'll throw you out on your ear."

Hart laughed again. "Good old Neil. So straightfor-ward. Come and have a drink, Neil, eh? I'd like to talk to you about the *Götterdämmerung*——"

"Sorry, Hart."

"You're very busy, eh? Well, so are all the little gods. This is the twilight of the little gods, Neil, let me tell you about it. The *Götterdämmerung*: The greatest myth of all. It's coming to life before our very eyes. Isn't that splendid, Neil, eh? The presumptuous little gods being struck down by the thunderbolts, the greedy little gods——"

"Very Wagnerian," Neil said. "You should say it to music." He tried to walk on. "I have to get back to work."

Hart blocked his way. "Oh, no. This myth, I assure you, goes beyond Wagner, way beyond. This is one of the oldest myths in history. It is recorded by civilization after civilization, how these gods—having proven them-selves unfit to exist as gods—were cast down and des-troyed. Many commentators——"

"I have to get to work," Neil repeated.

Hart moved aside. "Too bad. We could have had a most interesting talk. Some other time, eh? When you aren't so rushed? When there aren't so many thunder-bolts falling?"

"Maybe," Neil said. "I'll walk you to the elevators, Hart. And forget about seeing Mark."

Hart smiled. "Whatever you say, my dear chap."

At three o'clock the seventh salvo fell, the seven missiles scattering around Upper Broadway in New York, doing severe damage. Again, 143 other cities were attacked simultaneously. More than thirty of these sent official reports to InterCos by M-beam telling of unrest caused by the attacks, angry crowds assembling outside InterCos regional offices, clashes with police, et cetera. A large-scale riot was taking place in Chicago, where the stockyards and then the Loop had been hit by successive salvos.

On the Red circuit the Supreme Commander spoke about "a new and unusual and in some ways very alarming technology. He urged the Ministers to remain calm. "If we approach the problem judiciously, with confidence, we can be sure that we will prevail, we will overcome this monstrous threat to our lives, our hopes, our dreams."

The Turkish Minister called SecState Lowell to report that according to information received in Istanbul, very serious damage had been done to the Sahara and Lake Baikal installations. He had heard unconfirmed reports that similar damage had been done to Platform Alpha and to New Panama.

He called a few minutes later to report that no less than twelve battle wagons had been seen and heard taxiing across the Mediterranean for a water-assisted take-off. This information was confirmed by the Greek Minister.

The Arab Minister personally visited SecState Lowell, and was followed by the French, Belgian, and Italian Ministers, the Japanese Minister, the Pakistan, and Korean Ministers, and then by five of the Latin American Ministers.

In most major cities a frantic exodus was under way, but owing to indecision and lack of planning, roads were becoming blocked, and it was reported that as a result ambulances and fire-prevention services were often hindered in their efforts to reach bombed areas. The teleset in the Delegation office showed the major exits from New York City to be in a state of chaos.

In London, Paris, and Hongkong, warehouses and other buildings on the water front were reported burning as a result of contact with the metallic green fungus.

At a quarter to five in the afternoon, the Supreme Commander spoke again on the Red circuit, appealing for unity.

At five o'clock the eighth salvo fell.

At fifteen minutes past five Crandall returned to the Delegation office.

Neil was with SecState Lowell when Crandall walked in. He looked strange—exhausted and yet bronzed. His first words were, "Neil, lock the door."

Neil shut the door and locked it.

Lowell said, blinking with surprise, "Dwight. Dwight. Come and sit down. I thought we'd never see you again. Come and sit down."

Crandall flopped into his chair, looked at Lowell, looked at Neil, wiped his hand over his face as if it were covered with cobwebs, and grinned weakly. Then, as the grin spread, his features began to contort as if he were about to burst into tears.

"Man!" Lowell said, loudly and jovially: "You look as if you've spent a month in Florida. How the dickens did you get so sunburned?"

Crandall managed to check his emotion. He said in a flat voice, "We had quite a setup down there, you know. Ultraviolet, ozone . . . everything but bathing beauties."

Lowell chuckled. "I expected to see you looking pale as a ghost."

"I *feel* pale as a ghost," Crandall said. "I feel——" He stopped, and swung slowly in his chair to stare out of the window.

"Go on," Lowell said. He took his old place on the corner of the desk. "What has happened?"

"We've broken Werner," Crandall said. His face be-

164

gan to contort again. "Did you hear what I said? Did you hear me? We've broken Werner."

Lowell answered calmly, "I expected you would."

Crandall jumped up, shouting. "You *expected* we would. You——" He was glaring at Lowell in uncontrollable ferocity; and then, seeing the expression on Lowell's face, the smile of friendship, the smile of sympathy, he slumped back in his chair. He said, trying to smile himself, "Sure, sure. That's why the Federal Government pays me a salary. Do my job——" and he began to laugh.

"How much sleep have you had, Dwight?"

"Sleep, Mr. Secretary? Sleep?—We didn't sleep. We had to break Werner, and we did it, by God, Vernon and I did it. We didn't have time to sleep. But you know what? It's too late."

"Give me the outline. Then you can go and lie down."

"No time to lie down. Tell you what happened.—This afternoon, without informing us, Werner sent up the entire remaining fleet of battle wagons." His voice faltered. "Nineteen of them."

Lowell cried, "Without informing the Committee of Five."

Crandall nodded. His mouth twitched, and for a moment no words came out. "We heard—half an hour ago. Like this. Things were getting desperate down there. We had Dhevu on our side, but he kept hedging. Wouldn't come to any decision. Hsuen was shaky, but still with Werner. Balatov was one hundred per cent Werner. I can't go into all the details now, Mr. Secretary, don't ask me to——"

"Just keep going," Lowell said. "Tell me what you can."

"Werner was arguing for an all-out attack on the Ampiti. He kept saying it was impossible to negotiate, they were bombing our cities, they were going to poison us with these green algae, and so on. Therefore, be audacious. Attack with all our strength."

"Yes," Lowell said. "Yes. Then what?"

"On a decision like this he was supposed to obtain the consent of the full Committee of Five. He didn't wait.

He went ahead anyway. He ordered up a hundred and twenty squadrons of interceptors with all the f-weapons they could carry; and our remaining nineteen battle wagons. Two of the battle wagons developed reactor trouble en route. They're now trying to make their way back to the Mediterranean. But they were able to report what happened. The seventeen that went on were destroyed.—Lowell, they were destroyed before they could get into action. They weren't able to launch a single attack against the Ampiti. The Ampiti were waiting for them in some way—a space ambush, if you ever heard of such a crazy thing——" He stopped.

Neil's imagination began to picture the scene. There had been no descriptions of the Ampiti fleets hovering a thousand miles above Platform Alpha. If any InterCos craft had survived close contact, the reports had been kept secret. But the picture was easy enough to visualize: the huge battle wagons riding smoothly up into the blackness of space, the tiny bright Ampiti interceptors pouring down out of the sun——

"No," Crandall said, as if he could read Neil's thoughts. "It wasn't the sort of ambush we're used to. The full details haven't come in yet. But apparently they'd prepared clouds of gas, like the burning stuff on the water down here. And somehow the battle wagons were led into it." He stopped again.

Neil's imagination faltered and blacked out.

Lowell said, "All right, Dwight. Try to finish."

"That was it," Crandall said. His face had crumpled completely. "Even Balatov was convinced. We're now defenseless, except for interceptors. They may have gone, too, for all we know. We don't have the techniques, we're just a couple of hundred ants trying to fight a bull-dozer——" He was struggling to keep his head up. "It's a little late in the day, Mr. Secretary, but I have the honor to inform you that the Committee of Five will appeal to the Council of Ministers for a secret ballot to elect a new Supreme Commander."

"When?"

"As soon—as soon as possible."

"Will it be Vernon?"

"Hsuen came to me as we were leaving our hide-out and said he would support Vernon. Dhevu will too. I don't see how Balatov can hold out. He's plenty scared, with all our battle wagons gone. So, it will be Vernon. Or Werner."

"Werner!"

"Certainly. What did you think? He's going to fight on. He's still convinced he can be the architect of victory." Crandall began to laugh helplessly. "With his old black magic, I wouldn't be surprised if he talked the Council of Ministers into confirming him as Supreme Commander, dictatorship, no Committee of Five to give him trouble——"

"No," Lowell said firmly. "I've had conferences with half the Ministers already. They're scared out of their wits."

"Aren't *you?*" Crandall asked. "I am." All the blood drained from him, leaving his face saffron yellow, and he said, "I—I—I'm so tired," and slid down in his chair, with his head hanging loosely forward.

Neil sprang forward and supported him under the arms.

"I'll get Hooper," Lowell said. "The three of us can carry him to bed."

The teleset bell rang three times and the red light flashed on for a Priority One message. It was Dr. Werner, still in his splendid white uniform. He said with cool dignity, "The Supreme Commander requests all members of the Council of Ministers to be in their places in the Council Chamber promptly at seven o'clock tonight for a Secret Executive Session. In accordance with InterCos regulations, advisors and aides will be excluded from this session. I repeat the time and place. Seven o'clock: the Council Chamber."

The screen darkened.

Lowell said, "I thought it had been decided that the Council Chamber was too dangerous, because of all that glass. We were only to use the Concert Hall for Council meetings. What's the idea? Isn't glass dangerous any more? Or does that maniac hope the entire Council of Ministers will be wiped out if they dare to vote against him?"

Hart's words returned to Neil's mind. *Götterdämmerung.* There was some truth there. The twilight, the death of the gods, the final destruction of the wild dream. . . .

With astonishing callousness SecState Lowell began to slap Crandall's face. His voice was loud and harsh. "Come on, Dwight," he said. "Come on. Snap out of it, man. Wake up. You still have work to do. Wake up, wake up. You're not as soft as all that. Werner's still on his feet. D'you hear me? Werner's still on his feet. Wake up."

Crandall tried to move his head away from Lowell's swinging hands. Neil said angrily, "He's out cold. You can't wake him like that."

Lowell said, "I'll get him to that meeting if it's the last thing he ever does. There's a world at stake." He shouted, "Dwight!"

Crandall groaned.

"Let go of him," Lowell ordered. "Let him hit the deck. Maybe it'll wake him up.—Now get Hooper and we'll carry him to a shower. Hurry!"

Hooper looked up as Neil came to his desk and said, "Oh, say, Harrison, there's a file here that I'm sure is redundant——"

"We're all redundant," Neil said. "Come with me."

By a quarter to seven Crandall was more or less alive, shivering after his shower, his skin still yellow and his eyes still glassy. General Kirkland had been called in, and had massaged and pummeled Crandall's body until the man cried out in pain; Admiral Gould had concocted some powerful potion that had run down Crandall's throat and into his intestines like liquid fire. Nobody smiled. Nobody made any humorous remarks. It might be amusing in retrospect, if there was a future time to tell it, how Crandall was prepared for an InterCos session.

Lowell said to him, "What's this meeting, Dwight?"

"It's a S-secret Ex-executive——"

"That's right. What are you voting for?"

"A n-new—a n-new S-supreme Commander——"

"*Who* are *you* voting for?"

"V-vernon, of course. V-v-v-Vernon."

"Repeat that. Who are you voting for?"

Crandall cried, "D-don't be such a f-fool, Mr. Secretary. I know who I'm voting f-for. V-vernon. V-vernon, that's who." His head began to roll with weariness.

"Wake up!" Lowell cried; and Crandall said wretchedly, "I—I'm awake. I'm awake."

"You're going to do this right," Lowell said. "We can't take any chances. Kirkland——"

"Leave me alone," Crandall said. "For God's sake, leave me alone." Then he put his hand out and touched Lowell's arm and said, "Don't worry. This won't go wrong. I s-swear to you, it won't go wrong."

Lowell said, "See that it doesn't. They've been working over Vernon in the British Delegation, too. He's no better than you are. A fine pair of Delegates you make, by golly.—What happened to you down there? Dhevu and Hsuen are hardly awake. They can't get Balatov to open his eyes. What happened?"

Crandall stuttered, "We were fighting every m-minute. At the end—at the end, we were t-taking antisleep pills every hour on the hour." His head sagged again, and Lowell shouted, "Dwight!"

"Okay," Crandall said with a sigh. "O-o-o-okay." He looked at Neil in weak inquiry. "Mark?"

Neil said, "He's sick."

"F-fine," Crandall said. "That's j-just dandy. We put Vernon in, and then what?"

Lowell asked, "Neil, were you able to get hold of that girl?"

"Dr. Hewes? No, sir."

"Go and find her," Lowell said. "Find her and bring her here. With Mark out of action she's our only hope."

Neil said stiffly, "Yes, sir."

Lowell caught his eye. The older man's face had

169

softened. There was, at last, a hint of kindliness, of compassion, in that glance; it was tender and also sad, as if he were bidding farewell to somebody young whom he loved and might never see again. He was on the verge of speaking, but he swallowed the words and merely nodded and looked away.

Neil said, "Good luck, Dwight," and walked out.

He went to Room 6509, for a last glimpse of Mark. Bernie Ismay and Griff Luden were there, standing by the window, and Jordan Woolley was sitting on a chair, with his usual puzzled expression. The tableau was strange; the silence was alarming.

Neil's heart leaped with fear. He said anxiously, "Bernie——"

"He's in there," Ismay said in a chilly voice. "He's alive. Don't worry."

"Has something——" Neil began, and walked to the connecting door without waiting for an answer.

"Don't go in there," Ismay said sharply. "He drove us out. He was still in a coma, but he drove us out. Ask Griff. He was shouting like crazy, and then this blond guy walked in and Mark said to him 'So you've come at last,' and we were thrown out."

"Which blond guy?"

Jordan supplied the name. "Hart von Horstmann."

Neil leaped at the door.

Ismay caught him around the body and held on to him. He said, "Listen. You can hear them talking."

Neil heard the low murmur of voices.

Ismay said, "The odd thing is that Mark must still be in that coma. It's fantastic. This von Horstmann fellow walked in, and Mark said to him, 'So you've come at last' —but he couldn't have seen von Horstmann because he was unconscious, his eyes were still closed. And von Horstmann said something in German that I couldn't catch, and Griff couldn't catch either, and Mark said, 'Come closer to me, send the others away.' Von Horstmann walked over to him and took his hand, just like

170

that, and Mark shouted at us again, '*Get out.*' So here we are. Don't try to go in, Neil."

"So that was Benedict Arnold," Neil said, in wild realization, and left them. He had to find Libby now and stay with her, whatever came to the world, life or death; and suddenly, as he entered the elevator and went down to the great Arabian glass corridor, he was terrified of all this glass around him because it might slash him to pieces before he reached her.

The ninth salvo fell at seven o'clock, just as he left the building; the tenth fell only a few minutes later.

10

HE TURNED left when he came out of the blazing car park and began to walk across town to Fifth Avenue. He tried to compose himself, to walk loosely and without fear, at a swift yet comfortable pace; but he found it difficult to relax his body or even to control his breathing. The ninth salvo had fallen punctually, as expected. Then the pattern, the tempo of the bombardment had changed, the tenth salvo had come unexpectedly, before anybody was prepared, much too soon, much too fast, and his brain was tingling with anticipation. It was remarkable, he thought, how slavish the human system was even in circumstances like these, how agitated it became when any routine was disturbed, even the routine of death.

At first he walked as if he were fighting a strong wind, his head down, his body leaning forward, his fists clenched. Some relaxation of his muscles came only after he had walked several blocks. The night sky was brilliantly starry, innocent; it was hard to believe that it harbored implacable enemies. Somewhere ahead there was the faint clanging of fire alarms, the thin scream of police sirens; but otherwise the city seemed quiet, incredibly quiet and deserted as if all its inhabitants had suddenly vanished. This section, Neil recalled, near InterCos was generally quiet: a residential section, long rows of skyscraper apartment houses towering up like giants on parade, with well-kept lawns and children's playgrounds around the feet of each giant. Most of the InterCos secretariat lived in these handsome glass-walled buildings, breathed good air, looked out on vast horizons through big picture windows. Old Grandpa Moses had dreamed it, as his last dream of how the inhabitants of a great city should live. He would have been dismayed and surprised to learn that one day people would try to hide from those windows, try to cover them with wire mesh or heavy curtains or strips of adhesive tape, that they would try to blot out their horizons and shut out the stars.—*But these are strong buildings,* Neil thought, *and they stand well apart.* He thought of other cities, London, Tokyo, San Francisco, which were crowded with housing and where the missiles would always find targets.

Did the Ampiti, he wondered, *really intend to wipe out the human race? Was that their plan? Unrelenting bombardment for weeks and weeks? And the unrelenting spread of that burning green carpet until no human being could walk the streets?* He tried to visualize them now riding serenely in space over Platform Alpha, far beyond the range of an earthly counterattack, very secure in the possession of such weapons as the clouds of burning gas that had destroyed the seventeen battle wagons, calmly preparing the next salvo, and the next and the next—the eleventh, and the hundred and eleventh, and the thousand and eleventh. Were they antlike creatures, or were they even remotely human in appearance? It was odd. He had never considered this before, possibly because he had automatically assumed that they were in some degree humanoid. Like their targets. With brains, eyes, mouths, hearts? Presumably. And with emotions? Did they, for example, feel any emotions as they loaded their missiles? Did they, for example, chalk on the side of each missile some humorous, humanoid message. . . . *London, here we come,* or, *To New York with Love?*

He hurried on.

A few people passed him, also hurrying, fighting the same wind of fear. Men, hurrying to their families.

Girls, dominoed, stepping along with a clack-clack of high heels, seeking the refuge of their bachelorette apartments where they would lie on their pull-down beds, alone, waiting as the rest of the city waited, but alone.

He pitied all lonely human beings tonight.

All lonely girls in velvet dominoes.

Would the Ampiti continue, he wondered, *if they knew of these human beings, the men and women so fearful of each other, and the men and women fearful only for their children, and the lonely ones who could only fear sickeningly for themselves? Eleven missiles, to destroy a child's body, or a young girl's body, or the entwined bodies of a man and a woman crying aloud only for the other's safety? Would the Ampiti continue,* he wondered, *if they were aware that these were their targets?*

Why not, he answered himself, *why not? We ourselves have sought out these targets with great deliberation throughout our glorious long history. Man: the proud warrior. Now the Ampiti are copying man, the proud warrior.*

Perhaps this is what the Ampiti foresaw and feared, perhaps this is what they had to prevent. The soft, the lonely targets that man might seek on other worlds. Man. Man's dream. Man's empire. *To New York with Love.*

Somebody called to him in passing, "Some business, eh?" and he was so surprised, hearing a rough voice interrupting his thoughts, that for a moment he could not conjure up an answer. He turned, a few yards on, and called back, "Yes, some business. Some business." So it was. *How had they felt in Jericho,* he wondered, *as the trumpets sounded and the walls began to crumble? How had they felt when Constantinople was sacked and burned, when Carthage was razed to the ground, and the small, inefficient, antiquated gasoline-powered bombers dropped missiles on London and Berlin, Hamburg and Coventry, Liverpool and Cologne . . . Some business. An odd reaction,* he thought, *to Man's dream of targets. The dream of soft and tender and passive and quite anonymous targets that had inspired mankind for untold centuries. Targets that said in droll confusion* "Some business."

When he reached Third Avenue he realized what was happening to the city on this first full night of celestial warfare. The great roadway was completely choked with vehicles. Most of them had been abandoned. In some of them, families sat waiting helplessly, children looked out in wonderment. No further movement was possible. The cars, the families would have to stay here, the children would have to sleep here, under the bright lights of Third Avenue, at the feet of the giant apartment houses. And even if the cars could move again, gliding smoothly along with the road feelers gently slapping the speed governors (keeping each car exactly one and a half car lengths from the car in front) where would these people go? Where was safety to be found in this world? A farmhouse in Pennsylvania, a cabin in the Ozarks, or in the Himalayas? And then what? And how long would one have to wait? Some business, certainly.

A small girl with bright yellow hair poked her head out of a car window and called, "Hi."

"Hi, there."

"Are you all by yourself?"

"Yes," he answered. "All by myself."

"Gee," she said. "You're *brave*, walking all by yourself." She smiled at him wonderingly, as if he were a great hero.

He laughed.

Her father looked out and said apologetically, "We're stuck here," as if Neil might be wondering what he was doing, sitting here in a car with his wife and child.

Neil said, "It looks as if the traffic's stalled all the way up the Avenue."

"That's how it looks," the man said. "Never seen anything like it." And then, in a burst of irritation, "What are the police doing, for God's sake?"

"I don't know."

He began to walk on, and the little girl called, "I hope you get home soon."

He smiled. "Thanks."

Brave, he thought. *A hero.*

When he reached Lexington Avenue a policeman riding a small motor scooter on the sidewalk swung round and puttered back to him, balancing the machine awkwardly between his knees as he spoke. "Going home?"

Libby represented home. "Yes," Neil said.

"We're trying to keep folks off the streets," the policeman said. "Glass. It flies all over the place."

"I know."

"I only just realized it," the policeman said. "They shouldn't build glass cities like this if they're going to have wars, bombs and stuff.—Any news where you've come from?"

Neil, blank, diplomatic, said, "No."

"I hope we're hitting back," the policeman laughed. "And, so what if we're hitting back? There's still too much glass around here. Don't waste any time; get home while the going's good."

"I'll try."

The policeman raced his motor. "Found this old thing in the basement at the station," he shouted over the din, and went roaring off, grinning broadly.

Just before he reached Lexington Avenue a well-dressed woman of about thirty-five stopped him and said in a low voice, "Sir——"

"Yes."

"Let me walk with you, please. Let me walk with you, please." She was shivering.

He hesitated. Then he said, "Come along."

She walked a few paces at his side, and then took his arm tightly, possessively. She said, "Don't leave me. Please don't. Please don't leave me. Please. Please."

She sounded as if she were suffering from shock.

He said, "Where do you live?"

"Here. Right here. My husband's away. I'm all alone. Don't, please don't——"

"I'm walking a long way. I think you'd be wiser to go home." He felt wretched, speaking to her like this. She was an ordinary, well-dressed, terrified woman. Another lonely one.

"Let me walk with you," she said. "Please."

"Don't you have anybody you can go to?"

"My husband's in New Orleans. Don't leave me."

He repeated, "I have a long way to go. Honestly, I'm telling you the truth. Why don't you call up some of your friends——"

She burst into tears.

He said, "Come along, then."

But she stood perfectly still, the tears streaming down her face; and even when he said again, "Come along," she did not move. She looked as if all hope had left her. He said for the third time, smiling at her welcomingly, "Come along," and when she still did not move he walked on. He felt as if he had murdered something very weak, very helpless.

A target.

On the west side of Lexington Avenue a man wearing a white card on the band of his hat stopped him and said, "Where are you heading for, mister?"

"Fifth Avenue, Sixtieth Street."

"Married?"

"No."

"We need men. We're forming defense units to look after each block in this section. How about joining us?"

Neil said, "I'm sorry——"

"Look," the man said vehemently. "We *need* men. You can make yourself useful."

Neil pulled out his InterCos identification card. The man turned it toward the light and said, "Oh." He looked at Neil suspiciously. "You're on official business for InterCos?"

"Yes."

"I thought you people only traveled around in big snappy automobiles."

"Try to get an automobile through this," Neil said, waving at the unmoving cars in the roadway.

"That's right," the man said, and laughed. "I forgot. Okay, okay. You'd better make it fast, before the next lot comes down.—What's going on at InterCos, anyway?"

Neil shrugged his shoulders and smiled vaguely.

The man shrugged back at him.

In a way, he realized, he had forgotten about people. For a long time, he had simply lost awareness of them, the fifteen million people who existed one by one, separately, as individual beings, in this city; the two hundred and thirty-five million who existed separately, individually, in this nation; the untold millions outside, all biologically similar to himself and yet all separate. Now, in these stray encounters, he was becoming acquainted with the human race again.

He wondered, *If—for example—I stopped to tell that lonely frightened woman what has been happening at InterCos for these past four days, would it help her tears? Or this last man who spoke to me, who asked me what is going on at InterCos—if I dared to answer him, would he be more determined, more courageous? Would they— or the policeman on his motor scooter—appreciate what Werner, Dr. Werner, our Supreme Commander, has been trying to achieve for them, or Hsuen, or Balatov, or any of the others? No, obviously not, for InterCos is after all concerned with the very highest of high diplomacy (as the Ampiti could explain, forty thousand miles overhead). InterCos deals in matters far too complex, far too difficult for popular understanding.*

This deserted city.

Not really deserted. What was that last report? The astounding total of 94.211 per cent of all New York tele-sets are now tuned to the InterCos channel.

Astounding.

This poor deserted city. All Danāe to the stars.

At InterCos they are now starting to argue who shall be Supreme Commander. Werner is making a superb speech, and the Ministers are probably uneasy as they

178

listen to his eloquent and almost unanswerable arguments. Hsuen, Dhevu, will also speak eloquently, no doubt, if they can stay awake, Crandall will be eloquent in his own blunt way, Vernon in his quiet British way, if they too can stay awake. And no doubt Werner will be dropped and Vernon will become Supreme Commander of InterCos, the agency of inter-cosmic explorations and development, repository of Man's noblest dreams which —inexplicably, perhaps—do not seem to have enchanted the other occupants of the Universe as much as they have enchanted the Council of Ministers.

Poor city, poor city.

Libby.

Only four days ago, he recalled, in a world that was seemingly prosperous, confident and at peace, we were fighting among ourselves about those colonization quotas, who should have what on the barren surface of Mars; we were all wooing Dhevu secretly, and we were all striving to get a bigger slice of hard, stale, Martian cake. Would that lonely woman, who stood in the street crying, understand this high diplomacy?

And then, how cleverly we maneuvered to get the Beta time schedule postponed! Would the little girl in the car who called me a brave man understand this example of high diplomacy?

And the motor-scooter policeman, would he understand our diplomatic efforts on his behalf when we raised the issue of the convoy for the Beta sections? Very high diplomacy. Smart.

And when we met and agreed to have Mark talk to the Council of Ministers about the Voices, in order to make Dhevu more nervous, in order to postpone firing the final Beta sections, in order to reopen the question of colonization quotas, in order to prevent the Lord Hsuen from grabbing too large a piece of the Martian cake, in order to prevent Balatov from grabbing too much of the mineral rights and the construction allotments.

He thought, *It goes on and on and on.*

He thought, *I guess the Ampiti have fairly good rea-*

*sons for trying to keep us out of their space zones. Brutal
as they are, uncompassionate as they are.*

Wise characters, these Ampiti.

*But Libby, Libby, why should Libby suffer for all this
stupid treachery, and the little girl in the car who called
me a brave man?*

He had to keep up this monologue as he walked because every few moments there was a tremor through his
body, and he became aware of himself walking through
the streets alone and of the silence and the darkness
surrounding him. The fire alarms were still ringing in
the distance, but they only accentuated the immediate
silence; there was a glow of fires ahead and behind him,
but they only seemed to deepen the shadow in which he
was enveloped. The stench of the green fungus affected
his eyes, his skin, the mucous membranes of his nose,
like the fumes of sour vinegar. It was better to allow his
mind to ramble on so that he forgot his presence in this
glass city, so that he could walk unencumbered by fear.

Store windows filled with pretty things—bracelets,
watches, hats, furs, dresses, blouses, dominoes. Gray,
meaningless. The window of an art gallery, with three
oil paintings on display and a small piece of bronze.
Meaningless, now, all the joy gone from them. A window
exhibiting a single Chinese vase; a thousand years old?
Tell the Lord Hsuen. But how tragic! All that man had
created, all that was beautiful and heartfelt, all this was
not enough to outweigh the greed. Godlike; and yet so
untrustworthy. Lucifer.

A girl came toward him, smiled timidly through her
domino and paused; but he hardly noticed her—he
smiled politely in return and walked on. She called after
him, and when he looked round he saw that she had
taken her domino off so that he could see her face, a
gesture that was hardly different from disrobing completely, a gesture, in these circumstances, of frantic despair. "Go home," he said, "go home," terribly troubled
by the sight of her beckoning to him, waving the domino
in her extended hand. She wanted affection, she wanted

some warmth, some unimaginable pleasure before her life ended; even a stranger's arm would be welcome. Tonight might just as well be her bridal night as her funeral night.

He walked on. *InterCos!*

On Park Avenue, a small well-dressed man lurched over to him, beaming, and said happily, "Friend. Have a drink?"

"Thanks. But I'm in a hurry."

"Got it right here," the small man said, and felt through all his pockets. His eyes became puzzled. "Funny. Lost it."

"Too bad."

The man gurgled with laughter. "Drank it, that's what." He put his finger against the side of his nose and said solemnly, "Don't tell her you saw me," and trotted off. He remembered something, and cried, "Lovely night, eh?"

"Beautiful."

"Fireworks, too," the little man said. "Celebrating what? Must get another drink. Maybe my birthday."

Yes, Neil thought, *we are celebrating, but not your birthday, not your sad wedding anniversary. The fall of Lucifer, friend, the* Götterdämmerung. *There will probably be fireworks aplenty.—What was it Hart had said about the* Götterdämmerung?

Hart! He thought violently. *Hart von Horstmann! Hart and Mark! What was happening between those two? Ben—arn . . . ben—arn. . . . Was it possible that for all these months Hart had poured out to the Ampiti, step by step and step by step, the plans taking shape at InterCos for greater dominions? Hart, who like so many of his countrymen, carried always in his spirit a foreboding of the twilight of the little gods, the fall, the end of Lucifer's ambitions? Was it possible that the Ampiti had chosen him for their medium, or that he—consciously or unconsciously—had sought out the Ampiti?*

"So you've come at last," *Mark had said to him. Mark, his eyes still closed:* "So you've come at last." *And what had Hart answered, and what was happening now?*

For some reason his skin began to crawl, as if a new menace was closing in on him.

As he came to Madison Avenue he was stopped, once again, by a man wearing a white card in his hatband. The card, Neil saw, was lettered crudely *Warden*, and the man was middle-aged and red-faced. He was breathing heavily, as if he had been running.

Neil said, "InterCos," and produced his identification card. "I'm on official business."

"Sure it's official?"

"Yes."

"Live in this section?"

"No."

"Ah. All right, then. Sorry to hold you up."

Neil asked, "Are you forming defense units here?"

"Every able-bodied man we can get."

"I met one of your people on Lexington Avenue, doing the same job."

"That's good," the middle-aged man said. "Sensible. Glad to hear it. How was he making out?" He did not wait for an answer. He went on: "Everybody says *No* at first. Guys hesitate to leave their families. Then they realize, by golly, they can be a darn sight more useful if they're organized to meet these bombs than if they're sitting doing nothing in their apartments. Surprising: they're rolling in by the dozen now, by the dozen. We're forming stretcher parties, first-aid groups; even the women are being helpful, making bandages, checking food supplies, and so on and so on.—When you get back to InterCos, tell them we're doing our best, will you?"

"I certainly will."

He was a talkative, almost pompous middle-aged man; but standing here in the street with the white card in his hatband he was singularly impressive.

"Nasty business," he said. "Came as a shock to everybody. But, there you are. Once the shock wears off, human nature rises to the occasion, I think. Our biggest job now is to clear these streets so ambulances and fire trucks can get through. Can't see how we're going to do it, but I guess we will somehow." He looked ruefully up and down the avenue, and then smiled and held out his hand. "Well, nice talking with you. I'd better run along."

Neil took his hand, feeling warm about this man, suddenly feeling warm and affectionate to all humanity; and at this moment his ears roared with a black hurricane of wind and noise, the sidewalk seemed to tilt over, he was groveling on his hands and knees staring into the astonished eyes of the middle-aged man. The sky was reverberating with peal after peal of thunder and with the successive screams that always accompanied the thunder and that trailed up, up, all the way up to the hovering Ampiti fleets.

Then, with the eleventh thud there was a confused silence while the wind went whooping by; and the middle-aged man scrambled to his feet and muttered, "Good God," and began to run. He was not running away from something, Neil realized; he was running toward something, and it was urgently necessary to run with him—wherever he went—trying to reunite one's dazed mind and one's unmuscled body on the way, ignoring the cacophony that had followed the moment of silence, ignoring the fact that the island under bombardment was growing smaller and smaller.

Other people were running in the same direction, Neil saw: toward the devastation ahead, not away from it; men like the middle-aged man, with white cards in their hats, women with white cards pinned to their coats or their blouses. They were all in a hurry, they were all running grimly, and where they all had come from he could not guess. They poured through the smoke-filled avenue in an agony of haste.

The nearest missile had struck one of the giant apartment houses three blocks away, hitting obliquely about twelve stories above ground. The point of entry was quite clear—a jagged hole fifteen feet across, lit from behind by streamers of fire. Glass was still falling, detaching from window frames with a thin crack and then tinkling into splinters on the sidewalk. Walls and ceilings inside the building were collapsing, one after another; water was gushing out of broken pipes; and very high up there were human voices crying out, a strange frightening animal sound.

The middle-aged man pushed his way to the entrance. Neil stayed close to him. A crowd of men had already gathered there, breathing heavily, some of them with iron bars, some with pickaxes, some with stretchers. "What's happening?" the middle-aged man asked; and somebody answered, "Three guys went up to reconnoiter. They're trying the stairs. The elevators are out of commission."

They waited. They heard the noise of glass, the dull noise of metal, the noise of gigantic sheets of paper, all being torn and mangled and flung apart—as it were—off stage. A man came out of the building, already covered with grime, blood drying on his cheek, and said, "Six go up. No stretchers yet."

Six men ran into the debris-filled foyer.

The middle-aged man asked, "How is it up there?"

"Five floors smashed, I figure. The stairs are shaky. We'll have to throw planks across them."

"Planks," the middle-aged man said, "we didn't think of that." He smiled weakly at Neil. "At least, we're learning as we go along. Planks . . . ."

In the roadway groups of men were smashing in the side windows of locked cars and then steering them onto the sidewalks in an effort to clear a lane. Three policemen had arrived and were directing their operations. The fire bells and ambulance sirens were clamoring half a mile away. A man in a white coat climbed onto the roof of one of the stalled cars and shouted through a megaphone at the high wailing voices, "We're coming to you, don't panic, we're coming to you."

From the foyer a hollow voice called, "Ten men, ten men," and Neil and the middle-aged man hurried in.

The danger was that another wall might suddenly crumble, another ceiling, even the stairs themselves might give way. You worked up here in semidarkness, only a few flashlights to show where you were, with powdered plaster in your eyes and your mouth and your hair, your hands bleeding; and it was merely a matter of clearing a tunnel through the precarious places, an opening that would remain open and through which you could eventually crawl. You were nobody up here, only a link in a chain or a small lever. Somebody handed you a chunk of plaster and you handed it to the anonymous man behind you; and then you were handed a broken sheet of glass and you handed this behind you, too; and, gradually, you crept up and up and up, a few inches at a time, not daring to cough for fear the noise might bring an avalanche down on the line, you might dislodge some tiny fragment of material that was the keystone of the entire edifice. Every now and then you stiffened in terror as something rumbled overhead, something collapsed. It seemed endless and mad and hopeless, chunk after chunk of plaster being handed on and on and on; and then suddenly you heard the cry, passing it back gladly like a wonderful diamond: "Nurses! Stretcher-bearers!" and the women came swiftly and softly up, brushing past your body like gray ghosts, the stretcher-bearers following, stooping, trying not to soil their contraptions of wood and canvas, trying not to look sick at thoughts of what awaited them. But it was like reaching the peak of Everest, knowing that the way was open. And then the routine began all over again, reaching for chunks of plaster, of glass, of twisted metal, until eventually you yourself were crawling through the tunnel you had helped to make, and you found yourself in the incredible, the fantastic debris that only a short while ago had been a human habitation. The chain of men was still moving plaster, glass, metal, uncovering human beings who had been living here and who might still be alive here under the rubble; and the adrenaline surged into your veins until you were quite numb and quite beyond shock, and you worked very fast moving the rubble piece by piece by piece until the crumpled arm was uncovered, the battered head, the evidence of male or female. You called then in another voice, "Nurse! Stretcher-bearer!" and waited a moment, and passed on.

185

After an hour, or two hours—Neil could not even guess what the interval was this time—the twelfth salvo fell. It appeared to fall downtown. He thought, *There would now be more men working in rubble, in New York, in London, in Chicago, in Tokyo, in 143 cities.* And he thought of Hart. Hart and Mark.

The middle-aged man said in a choked whisper, "Come on. Let's get out of this," and Neil followed him faithfully back through the tunnels, through the stinking debris of the apartments, through more tunnels and down the cracked flights of stairs to the street.

"Air," the middle-aged man said. "Stuff got in my lungs." He began to cough heavily, his head down.

Neil stood at his side, looking around at the bodies lying on the sidewalk, some dead, some alive; at the women and the internes in white jackets hurrying to and fro; at the ropes dangling from the blackened hole in the giant building. It was like a battlefield, the aftermath of a battle: a confusion of litter and bodies and cars, with a hundred headlights illuminating the scene.

The middle-aged man had lost his hat. His clothes were torn, one sleeve of his coat was ripped out, and he was splattered with white dust; but it seemed to Neil that he now wore a very magnificent uniform, very magnificent indeed.

He stopped coughing.

"Feeling better?" Neil asked sympathetically.

"Yes."

"Well, I'd better run along, I guess."

The middle-aged man turned and stared at him, and then said with a smile of recognition, "I remember. You're with InterCos. Just passing by, weren't you?"

"That's right."

For a moment the middle-aged man was silent. He was staring at the people lying on the sidewalks, at the people tending to them. "You know," he said ruminatively. "We can lick this thing. They can throw all the bombs they like at us. We'll still make out somehow."

"I hope so."

The middle-aged man shook Neil's hand. "I'd better

186

see about getting those planks. Hope we'll meet again soon." He looked up at the sky. "Planks! In this day and age! What do you know about that?" He clucked his tongue and bustled off.

Then a few yards away he remembered something. He turned and called back to Neil, "Oh, incidentally——"

"Yes?" Neil called in reply.

"Thanks for helping." The middle-aged man smiled at him through the smoke. "Thanks a lot."

In the Council Chamber at InterCos the result of the secret ballot was announced by the acting President. The session had been stormy. Earlier, during the debate, the Polish and the French Ministers had been ejected from the assembly for screaming abuse at each other; the Hungarian Minister had threatened to withdraw, the Arabian and the Turkish Ministers had eyed each other in a threatening manner.

There was silence as Vernon walked to the podium to make his first speech as Supreme Commander. He carried with him a few pages which had been hastily written by Locke and Lowell, beginning with due ceremony, "I must thank the Council of Ministers for the great honor that it has bestowed upon me"; but when he stood before the Ministers he made no use of this text. For several moments he did not speak, and appeared to be summoning up resources to strengthen his weary body; and then, with his hands clasped tightly behind his back, he said, "There is no need for me to stress the peril which we face. You are now all fully aware of it. Nor shall I attempt to fasten responsibility for this peril on any individuals in this assembly. We are all in some measure responsible. We had only to open our history books to see the inevitable results of aggrandisement and conquest. I will not dwell on this point."

He unclasped his hands and gripped the sides of the reading desk. Some of the Ministers were pale, some were scowling. He went on, still not paying any attention to the draft in front of him, "We must now revise our estimates of ourselves. We must regard ourselves in an entirely new perspective. In this new, unflattering, but very accurate perspective we will see ourselves as we truly are: a small planet. A ridiculously small planet, in comparison with the other masses in the Universe. And as a small planet, an almost microscopic speck of dust, we have succeeded in arousing the hostility of overwhelming forces who do not like our manners or our methods, and who are ranged securely against us. There is no possibility of victory against them. There is every possibility that they will take this opportunity to wipe us out as some kind of pest, some kind of cosmic nuisance. It is also my view that we cannot attempt any kind of delaying maneuver, for gaining time will not help us. We cannot employ new tactics, we cannot seek for any subterfuges to distract the attention of these antagonistic forces. In my opinion we can only save whatever is possible of our civilization by employing an unaccustomed device: the total honesty of total helplessness. That, my friends, is the situation."

His voice became a little louder. "We must find means to give proof of our honesty and our helplessness. Very well. The last order promulgated by our former Supreme Commander was for a complete blackout over the whole of our globe. I hereby rescind that order. Instead, I shall ask that every light in every city and in every village shall shine out tonight. All windows shall be uncurtained. Let the Ampiti see us clearly. We have two battle wagons left, out of our ultimate defenses. As fighting equipment they are useless. Very well. I order that they shall take off as soon as possible, with searchlights and all other lights switched on. Interceptors standing on the decks of these battle wagons shall be floodlit with their wings in retracted position."

He leaned forward, speaking with sharp emphasis. "That is the beginning. More light. More light. More light on everything around us. Let us see if we can go on from there."

He ended abruptly. "The Committee of Five will meet in fifteen minutes to consider any other measures that may help to insure global safety. I will be present." He picked up the notes which he had not used, and then stood uncertainly with one hand on the rail of the podium; not as though he was awaiting the Ministers' reactions to his speech, but as though he was too tired to move from this place.

SecState Lowell, watching the assembly, saw that the Ministers were too stunned to show even the usual courtesies following a speech by a newly elected President and Supreme Commander. There was a timid spatter of applause, but it died quickly. The Roumanian Minister rose and began aggressively, "Mr. President," but Balatov pulled him down at once and whispered angrily in his ear. Madame Ai-Wen-Tai was whispering in the ear of the Lord Hsuen. Dhevu's sister was weeping quietly into a small hand-woven cotton handkerchief.

They're whipped, Lowell thought. *They're whipped, and they are forced to accept Vernon's policy. And yet, if our skins are saved tonight, how long will it be before the chicanery starts again?*

He knew the answer to this; and he felt very bitter.

In silence, Vernon stepped down from the podium.

On the sixty-fifth floor Bernie Ismay thought he heard his name called, and he opened the door of Room 6508 and looked inside. Mark Harrison and Hart von Horstmann were sitting as they had been earlier, their hands locked together. As far as Ismay could tell, Mark was in a coma, but still breathing, still alive. The eyes of the young man were open, but apparently he was not aware of Ismay's presence. He was speaking in a whisper, not to Mark, but in a strange way *through* him. He was speaking, Ismay guessed, in German, a language Ismay did not understand. It was a flowing, rhythmical whisper, sounding like something from a song or a poem.

"Ismay," Mark muttered. "Ismay. Are you here?"

"Yes," Ismay said, and hurried to his side.

"Don't worry," Mark said thickly. His eyes were tightly closed. "Don't worry. Be all right now. Ampiti. Be all right."

"What are you saying?" Ismay asked. He bent low to listen.

"Call Evelyn. Call Evelyn."

Ismay felt his pulse and went running out. He said violently to Griff Luden, "Go in there. Stay with him. I have to get Evelyn."

Hart's voice rose wildly. "Light! More light, more light! They'll see us now. They'll see we've been telling the truth—"

Ismay cried to Luden, "Turn that young maniac out of there, Griff. Throw him out."

Griff called a moment later, "I can't loosen their hands."

Then he called in horror, "Something's happened. Bernie, something's happened. I think Hart's gone stark, staring mad."

Neil walked northward along Madison Avenue, through the area of destruction caused by the eleventh salvo. Everywhere there was the same activity. Stalled cars were being pushed onto sidewalks, policemen and civilians were on duty at every intersection, women and orderlies were tending the injured, covering the dead. People were pushing handcarts piled with cans of food. Groups of children and elderly folks were being led to shelter.

Those eleven missiles had all fallen into the east. On Fifth Avenue there was little evidence of the blind bombardment; a few broken windows, but little debris, no crumpled bodies, no women holding bowls of water. *It would come, no doubt,* Neil thought; *it would come.* But he walked without any fear now; slowly—because he was tired—but loosely, easily. His mind seemed clearer, too; and it might have been a false lucidity, the result of his fatigue, but he felt as though he understood many things which he had never understood in the past.

Two opposing principles had met, he saw. On the one hand you had the Ampiti, defending their own concept of existence, cruelly and ruthlessly. On the other hand you had the human race. And they had met in a conflict that should never have occurred if humanity had only been true to itself. For humanity (he felt) was symbolized not by Dr. Werner, not by any of the lofty diplomats of InterCos, not even Lowell or Crandall or Vernon, but by that middle-aged man who was now searching for planks to bridge the ruins for which he had taken full responsibility. Humanity, in a torn coat, could be very splendid, very heart-warming. It had the power to be noble in adversity, to defy death, to defy catastrophe, to defy these showers of bombs coming unheralded from the sky, to be kind and gentle, frightened and yet courageous.

He was very proud to have become acquainted with the human race again. It was a pity this had to happen, but in effect the circumstances were not really new. Men and women had been forced to endure all this before; only in all probability (he assumed and was virtually convinced) this was the final purgatory. He could understand now why the Ampiti had not used any fission weapons which would destroy each city at a single blow. Humanity was being forced to run a gauntlet that would be burned into the race memory—if any fragment of the race survived. This was the last lesson.

He had no idea what decisions were being made at InterCos, or by the commander of the fleets overhead. He could only wonder as he walked when the next salvo would fall, the thirteenth, the unlucky thirteenth, maybe; he could only wonder how long this purgatory would go on.

He came to Sixtieth Street, and his heart moved with thankfulness when he saw that the apartment house had not been harmed. He went up in the elevator, rang the doorbell, and the door opened silently at once. Libby stood facing him. She wore no domino.

She said in terror at the sight of him, "Neil!" Her hand rose to her breast. "Neil. Are you hurt?"

"No."

"Thank God." She burst into tears and flung her arms around him. The little scaly poodle crouched on its forepaws, giving tiny excited barks.

191

They stood in the doorway holding each other, and then Libby said, crying and laughing, "Matilda, be quiet. It's Neil. I told you Neil would come today, I told you."

Neil said, "I've been calling you all afternoon. Were you out?"

She turned her head. "Yes." Then she looked at him again, making an effort to smile, to blink back her tears, to sound gay and lighthearted and just normally affectionate. But when he was inside the apartment and the door was closed she whispered in uncontrollable fear, "Your hands are scratched, Neil. And your forehead." She touched the dried blood on his forehead. "What happened? Tell me."

"Nothing serious." He sat down heavily on the settee. There were no fish swimming in the long fish tank, he noticed.

She said, "Let me take your jacket. It's covered with dust." He moved his arms clumsily as she pulled it off. She said, "Sit back, Neil. Make yourself comfortable," and left the room.

He picked up the scaly poodle. It licked his chin and the side of his neck, and when he scratched lightly between its ears it sat up panting with pleasure. Its eyes were exceedingly bright, and he could feel its heart beating very rapidly.

Facing him, Libby's teleset was switched on, and he could see one of the InterCos announcers on the screen and hear a murmur of words. The sound was turned low. He caught the name Vernon, and the title Supreme Commander, and nodded to himself because it confirmed what he had hoped and expected. But he was not really excited by the victory. It might have happened in another life, perhaps in a co-existent life of strange noise and strange turmoil. His mind was distracted by a dozen different thoughts, and his body was aching as if it had emerged from a terrible ritual of scouring. Every bone was bruised, every inch of skin was painful.

Libby returned with warm water and towels. She put them down at his feet; and as she knelt he said, "No, no,

192

you mustn't do that," but he could not move away from her.

She was very soft and gentle. She cleaned his hands, and as she raised herself to dab at his face he kissed her, and was surprised to feel tears on her cheeks.

He thought he would try to distract her, and he said with a queer laugh, "Do you know why I am here?"

She looked at him in surprise.

"Not just because I had to be near you," he said. "Not just because I love you. I'm here on official InterCos business."

"Here?" she asked. "You're *here* on InterCos business?"

"Lowell sent me. He wants you to come and work at InterCos. He needs your help on semantics. That's why I was calling you all afternoon."

She said quietly, "I'll be very happy to work at Inter-Cos."

He asked curiously, "Where were you when I called?"

"Out."

"But where?"

Her lips tightened. She took the little poodle off his lap and carried it to a pillow on the floor in a corner of the room. She said, "Go to sleep now, Matilda," and it curled its thin body, looking up at her piteously.

When she returned he said, "You don't have to tell me if you don't want to."

She said, "I was out with Matilda."

He did not ask anything more. He sensed from her manner that something profound was involved in this brief sentence, and she would either tell him or not tell him.

She repeated in a calm flat voice, "I was out with Matilda, Neil. We spent the afternoon walking up and down the sidewalk outside the animal hospital."

"Why?" he asked. "Is Matilda sick?"

She said, "I took Matilda and all my tropical fish." Her voice faltered. "I couldn't bear to think of them suffering, I was going to have them all destroyed, but I couldn't bear to, I couldn't make up my mind, I didn't have the courage——"

193

She pressed her face against his shoulder. It was another odd happening, he thought, it was like the man calling to him in passing *"Some business,"* odd, surprising, droll, and yet containing in itself all the tragedy and the heartbreak of tens of thousands of years of man's existence. The animal hospital.

He said, "Poor Libby."

"I took the fish in," she whispered. "But I couldn't part with Matilda. I thought, minutes are precious to Matilda. I thought, if we're going to be . . . killed . . . wiped out . . . she might as well have it happen in my arms. And, Neil—it might not happen after all, there might be some miracle. . . . I just walked up and down with her all afternoon, crying. I was so ashamed of myself."

Very odd, he thought. *Very droll.*

And it was so unbearably droll that he stood up and walked away from her to the big picture window. The curtains were drawn. He touched the button that opened them, and stood looking out at the dark city.

Libby said hesitantly, "There was an instruction from InterCos earlier this evening that all curtains were to be kept closed. We're not permitted to show any light."

"It makes no difference," he said.

She did not speak again.

He stood in silence. How droll, yes, how laughable, in the climactic moment of human history, this girl's misery over the fate of a shivering little scaly poodle! A little biological freak, with only a few more months to live in any event. How odd, Libby carrying it in her arms all afternoon, weeping over it, unable to part with it, like a mother carrying a child.

The human race too, he thought, *was a biological freak, shivering in the darkness tonight, awaiting extinction in incredulous horror. There should be a giant Libby who could hold the entire human race in her arms, a greater Libby to weep and console all human beings. It was a pity that mankind had no gods left. Not even Prosperpine. Not even Mary.*

And yet, there was the man in the torn coat; that pompous talkative middle-aged man. . . .

Libby came and stood beside him, not touching him. *This is humanity, he thought, here in this room at my side, and down there in the darkness surrounding me, in the frightened and shattered city. Millions and millions of odd creatures, so droll, so wonderful, so lovely, so absurd. Is it possible that all of us carry within us that gray streak of treachery together with that bright red streak of love?*

Libby. And this dark city. And the dark cities all over this earth. I am bound to them, and they are all bound to me. And at last, literally, in and through this darkness I can see it. Not kings, nor principalities . . . but I myself, and they themselves. All waiting for the next salvo, perhaps the decisive salvo; and all of us bound together by our common heartbeats.

She said, scarcely interrupting him, "I think I'll make some coffee. Would you like some, Neil?"

"Yes. Please."

"And then we'll leave for InterCos?"

He turned to look at her. "Yes," he said. Her face was very pale without the velvet domino, very smooth. *There were no barriers any more,* he thought. *There will never be any barriers between us any more: however long any more might turn out to be.*

She did not go to make the coffee at once. She slipped in front of him, cutting off his view of the dark city. "Must you stand here?" she asked.

He was conscious of the softness of her body. "Mustn't I stand here?" he smiled.

"I've had the teleset on all evening," she said. "Every few minutes somebody at InterCos gives a speech about staying away from glass——"

He swung her aside, so that her soft body could not act as a shield against any driving slivers. She cried, "Oh Neil, oh my darling, oh Neil," and he had to hold her tightly for several minutes before she was able to leave him and go to the kitchen.

He remained where he was, staring out.

Dark city, he thought. *Glass city. The middle-aged man in the torn coat, and the girl who took off her domino to call to me, and the little man who thought the fireworks were for his birthday—what does InterCos have to offer you, and what do I have to offer you? I wish we could have been better together. It is probably too late, but I wish. . . . And Lowell probably feels the same; and perhaps Balatov is thinking with deep affection of his people, and perhaps the Lord Hsuen is hearing the sad songs of the little maidens in the villages and the cities of his country, and Dhevu, too, Dhevu the Uncertain.*

I should like the world to go on, he thought, *for your sakes as much as my own, droll absurd gray-streaked oddities that we are, I should like the world to go on without any more salvos from the indignant Ampiti; and perhaps we could have newer and brighter and more human dreams. . . .*

Libby was at his side again. He moved back with her. The next salvo might fall at any moment.

He said, "Is the coffee ready?"

"Not yet. In a few moments." She sounded perturbed. "Did you hear the last InterCos announcement?"

"About Vernon?" he asked. "About Vernon becoming Supreme Commander?"

She said, "No." She took his arm. She said, "No, this was to order everybody to switch on all their lights and open all their curtains. Did you hear it?"

He shook his head.

"How strange," she murmured. "I wonder why?"

They stood side by side looking out; and, as they watched, the darkness began to sparkle all over the city. It was like watching violins breaking into a dancing pizzicato; and suddenly the city was blazing with light.

He thought his heart would burst.

Libby's fingers were tight against his skin, as if she would never let go of him now.

"How beautiful," Libby said. "Oh! How wonderful."